*Frowning slightly, a tall, slender young man draped in a* pale gray floor-length leather coat leaned over the counter, staring at the delicate fox mask locked under glass. His left hand was jammed in the pocket of his black dress-slacks, pulling his coat back and showing a dark gray sweater over broad chest and flat belly. His long platinum-blond hair, combed straight back from the deep peak of his brow and bound by a silver clasp into a long white tail, fell over his shoulder and spilled across the counter.

Rusty stared at the spill of pale hair and his heart slammed in his chest. He wiped his damp palms down his knee-length black apron. "You wanted to see me?"

The blonde turned. Warm cinnamon eyes framed in long black lashes peered at him from under straight dark brows. Sharp cheekbones and a strong jaw-line defined his aggressively masculine face, but the lush fullness of his mouth and the ivory-pale color of his skin belonged in a high-class modeling magazine.

His eyes widened. "My God..." The voice was soft, yet deep and very masculine. The lush lips rose to curve into a sinful smile. "I've been looking everywhere for you."

Rusty's stomach clenched in alarm. He knew that smile. He knew that *face*. It was the same one from his dream. But that couldn't be right... "Do I know you?"

Tempestuous
A Shounen-ai Fantasy
Copyright © 2006 Morgan Hawke
ISBN: 1-55410-680-X
Cover art by Eiris Key
Cover Design by Martine Jardin

Published by eXtasy Books, a division of Zumaya Publications, 2006
Look for us online at:
www.zumayapublications.com
www.extasybooks.com


Hawke, Morgan, 1963-
    Temptestuous / Morgan Hawke ; editor, Stefani Kelsey.


Also available in electronic format.
ISBN 1-55410-680-X


    I. Kelsey, Stef  II. Title.

PS3608.A83T44 2006        813'.6        C2006-901603-8

# Tempestuous

## ~ A Shounen-ai Fantasy ~

## Morgan Hawke

*For*
*Erin S.*
*My Secret Weapon*

# ~ One ~

HE THRASHED IN HIS SHEETS, DREAMING...

Smooth skin moved under his palms, and hair swept across his bare skin. Silver hair... Long silver-blond hair spilled through his fingers. Arms closed around him and a hot mouth pressed against his chest. A skilled tongue circled and lapped across his nipple. "Do you want...?"

Fire sparked and spilled downward, making his heart pound, his blood race and his cock fill. "Of course I want, idiot."

A pale exquisite face with high cheekbones looked at him from half-closed, red-gold, copper eyes under straight dark brows. "It will cost you."

Cost? A shiver broke across his skin. "What do you want, my soul?"

Framed in black lashes, the red-gold gaze focused on him with feral heat. "And your heart. I want your heart and soul." A lush mouth made for sin curved upward into a breathtaking smile. "Will you give them to me?" Long nails bit deliciously into his ass.

"Sure." He moaned shamelessly, clutching at the warm body that held him close. "It's not like I'm using them."

Hands caught his face. "Kiss me." Lips covered his. A tongue plunged in to taste, to explore with velvet strokes.

He moaned straight into the hot, wet mouth...

Strong hands clutched at his shoulders, urging him onto his back, and his knees were pushed up. A palm swept down his belly to close on the length of his painfully hard cock.

His spine arched, pressing his cock into the palm that held him,

1

*and he moaned into the mouth locked onto his. He pulled from the kiss. "Wait..."*

*"No." The hand stroked him, down and then up, slowly and then faster. "I've waited long enough."*

*Heat flashed through his body. His balls tightened with urgency, and his upraised knees jerked in reflex. He locked his arms around the pale, smooth back and broke from the kiss, gasping. "I'm going to... I'm going to cum."*

*"Yes!" Fingers knotted in the hair at the back of his neck, tugging his head back, exposing his throat. Copper eyes stared hard into his. "Yes, you will." The silk of all that silver hair spilled across his chest. Teeth raked across his throat, then a wicked tongue stroked the pulse beating under his skin. "You will come—to me." The teeth bit down, hard.*

*He gasped, shocked. Heated lightning raged through him. His body bucked hard. He screamed, and came.*

Rusty snapped awake, his body shaking, his shouts echoing in his ears. He gasped for breath, blinking in the darkness of his bedroom. He shoved the sheets away from his sweaty skin, and discovered that they were little more than rags. He'd ripped them apart. On top of that, thick gobs of hot wetness cooled on his belly and chest. He'd cum all over himself. He rose from his bed. "Damn it!"

He stumbled in the dark to the bathroom and turned on the light. He winced in the sudden brightness and looked into the mirror over the sink. His shoulder-length, sweat-darkened hair gleamed red under the bright light. White, sticky gobbets were spattered up his belly and onto his chest. He groaned. The stuff was everywhere. A washcloth was not going to do a damned bit of good. "Shit..."

He stepped into the small, glassed-in shower stall and turned on the water. In minutes, the bathroom was full of steam. He jammed his head under the near-scalding spray.

A wet dream... What the hell had brought that on? He grabbed for the soap and started scrubbing. The person in the dream wasn't someone he knew. He damned sure would have remembered meeting a woman that hot. And what was up with the biting?

Rusty shut off the water and stepped from the shower. Yawning, he reached for the towel, glancing back into the mirror. He froze, staring at his reflection. His green eyes widened. A thin line of scarlet was running down his throat.

*What...?* He shoved his dark, wet hair away from the side of his throat and leaned closer to the mirror, peering at his scars. Two finger-long lines and two tiny marks beneath them, clearly from upper and lower fangs, marred the side of his throat right below his left ear. Something had bitten him in the woods during his senior year of high school. He still couldn't remember anything of what had happened.

Yesterday the scars had been pale and faded, but overnight they had turned bright red. Blood trickled down his neck. "What the hell is this?" He pressed his fingers against the wounds.

In the dream, he'd been bitten—right there.

"No..." He stared at the blood smeared on his fingertips, and a cold sweat erupted all over his body. "Dreams don't do shit like this!" He slammed his fist down on the edge of the tiny sink.

The sink shook. A soft crack and then a tiny chinking sound caught his ear. He looked down. In the sink, a small circle of porcelain the size of a large coin slid to the bottom, leaving a bare spot of cast iron where his fist had landed.

"Ah, shit." His short temper had struck again. "Damn it..." He knew better than to cut loose like that. He looked at his hand, opening and closing it. Nothing, not even a bruise, though he'd used enough force to chip the porcelain in the sink.

He wiped his hands down his face. "Why does all the weird shit happen to me?"

On top of the mysterious scars, he was too damned strong. With his wiry build, he shouldn't be anywhere near as physically strong as he was—stronger than guys with a lot more muscle mass.

It was a frikkin pain in the ass. He had to be careful all the damned time. He tended to accidentally break things and could cause bruises just by holding on to someone too tightly. Sex had to be handled with extreme care.

His lip curled. *What sex?* He hadn't had any real sex in nearly a year. He sighed. It was just easier to go home and take care of himself than chance hurting someone.

He snorted. Probably why he'd had that wet dream.

But why was his throat bleeding? He picked up a cloth and dabbed at the blood seeping from his scars. What the hell had happened to him in the woods all those years ago?

An image of sunlight through autumn leaves, then long silver-blond hair and red-gold eyes danced on the edges of his mind.

"No…" That couldn't be right. He was mixing his dream with what little memory he had. He'd been bitten by some-*thing*, not some-*one*. Something with fangs. Some wild animal, not a person.

Rusty dried his hands without looking into the mirror again, and stalked out of the bathroom. "I need…a cigarette."

Naked, he padded into the hall. Turning right, he stepped into the spare room—his personal workshop—and flipped on the light. His cigarettes were on the worktable before the window. He walked over, picked them up and lit one. He took a drag, staring at the folding doors of the closet. He scraped his fingers through his sleep-tousled hair.

Frowning, he walked over to the closet and shoved open the folding doors, exposing the massive battered dresser he kept in there. He jerked open the middle drawer, rummaged and pulled out the long, smooth oak box. He opened it. Nestled on a scrap of red velvet, the shining black fox stared at him with metallic gold eyes, grinning with white-fanged amusement.

He still had no clue where he'd found the skill to carve the tall ears, the slanted eyes and the grinning muzzle, or what had possessed him to carve a fox mask in the first place. All he remembered was that the mask was connected to the nightmares he'd suffered right after the accident.

He frowned, staring at the mask. He couldn't recall anything from any of the horrific dreams. He remembered having them, but he couldn't remember a damned thing from them, other than that they had stopped once the mask was completed.

Not that it was a bad thing. He sucked on his cigarette, then blew smoke. Just one more unsolved mystery in his messed-up life.

# ~ *Two* ~

*F*ACING THE FLOOR-TO-CEILING FRONT WINDOWS, RUSTY HUNCHED OVER the old 1963 cream and green Singer sewing machine. It was warm from the furnace in the basement workroom but beyond the windows, the winter-bare trees rocked in a breeze that was barely above freezing.

Rusty repositioned the heavy, opalescent white silk and pressed his foot against the power pedal under the machine's amazingly small old-fashioned treadle cabinet. His knees barely fit under it. The zipping needle's high-pitched hum whirred in his ear and his jaw tightened. The Japanese robe he was battling to sew was not cooperating. The slippery silk was almost as hard to work with as freaking velvet.

Thumps and squeaks announced someone coming down the stairs.

Rusty scowled. *Not now, damn it!* The last thing he needed was an interruption.

"Rusty?" Halfway down the creaky wooden stairs set against the right foundation wall, Des peeked under the edge of the basement ceiling, her long dark braid falling over her shoulder and her round glasses reflecting the light from the long fluorescents dangling in three neat rows from the ceiling. "Rusty, can you come upstairs?"

Rusty took his foot off the machine's pedal, stopping the needle. "Des, I'm right in the middle of this." He used his left thumb to flip up the lever on the back of the machine to lift the presser foot from the silk, then tugged gently at the crushingly expensive handpainted material, smoothing it straight.

"I know, I know, but it's about your mask."

He stopped, a cold chill shivering along his spine. "My mask?"

"Yeah, that awesome fox you did. Somebody wants to see it."

Rusty used his left thumb to drop the lever on the back of the machine, setting the presser foot very carefully back down on the silk. He still couldn't figure out how his mask had ended up in his knapsack. He hadn't even realized he'd had it with him until it fell out onto the floor.

Des had been charmed at once, and had reached for it. Rusty had snatched it right out from under her fingers and locked it away in one of the display cases. He didn't like people touching it. The mask was...personal. It was like they were touching an intimate part of him. "Tell them it's not for sale."

"I did, but the customer wants to meet the guy that made it."

*Damn it!* If it wasn't one thing, it was another. He set his brow down on his forearm, took a deep breath and sighed. She was a good kid, and didn't deserve his temper. "Des..."

"Please, Rusty? The customer is being... impatient."

Rusty clenched his jaw. There wasn't a whole lot Des couldn't handle in the shop, but she was only a teenager and she had a 'nice' streak about a mile wide. If she said they were being impatient, then they were probably being obnoxious. As the shop's manager, handling rude, obnoxious customers was Rusty's job.

He lifted the presser foot from the silk and set his project carefully to the side. "Fine, I'm coming."

Des grinned. "Great! Thanks!" She turned and clattered back up the stairs.

Rusty checked to make sure his project wouldn't slither off the sewing table and onto the floor, then glanced around the bright chaos of his dresser-and-cabinet-lined workshop.

Concept sketches and designs from a million costuming projects hung on every available inch of wall space. The center of the room held the huge cutting table crammed with drawers. Before the windows at the far end was an old industrial leather stitcher mounted on the high worktable. Beside it was the surger for fast finishes and quick jobs. He set his palm on the machine before him, his pride and joy, the old Singer.

The workroom was a catastrophe of perfect order. Absolutely everything was in its proper—if crowded—place, from the smallest straight pin to the heavy bolts of fabric and the cloth-enshrouded clothing racks lining the back wall. His world was exactly as it should be.

Except for the interruption waiting for him upstairs.

Rusty turned his back on the sewing machine with his latest project and climbed the old wooden stairs along the foundation wall. He tugged at the collar of his black turtleneck. The gauze he'd taped on his throat was itching.

At the top of the stairs, he stood in the doorway and scraped his hands through his shoulder-length hair, surveying the merry insanity of the costume shop's crammed showroom. Des, dark-haired, lanky and bespectacled, was nowhere in sight.

At the main counter, stretching along the left wall hung with hundreds of Halloween masks and only three long strides away from the door, was the interruption.

Frowning slightly, a tall, slender young man draped in a pale gray floor-length leather coat leaned over the counter, staring at the delicate fox mask locked under glass. His left hand was jammed in the pocket of his black dress-slacks, pulling his coat back and showing a dark gray sweater over a broad chest and flat belly. His long platinum-blond hair, combed straight back from the deep peak of his brow and bound by a silver clasp into a long white tail, fell over his shoulder and across the counter.

Rusty stared at the spill of pale hair and his heart slammed in his chest. He wiped his damp palms down his knee-length black apron. "You wanted to see me?"

The blond turned. Warm cinnamon eyes framed in long black lashes peered at him from under straight, dark brows. Sharp cheekbones and a strong jaw-line defined his aggressively masculine face, but the lush fullness of his mouth and the ivory-pale color of his skin belonged in a high-class modeling magazine.

His eyes widened. "My God…" The voice was soft, yet deep and very masculine. The lush lips rose to curve into a sinful smile. "I've been looking everywhere for you."

Rusty's stomach clenched in alarm. He knew that smile. He knew that *face*. It was the same one from his dream. But that couldn't be right… "Do I know you?"

The blond guy straightened to stand a full head taller than Rusty. He brushed the long silver tail over his shoulder, letting it fall down his back. His brow lifted. "You don't remember me?"

Rusty stiffened. "Remember…you?" His neck ached. He clenched his hand into a fist to keep from reaching for the throbbing scars. Beneath the collar of his shirt, he felt hot wetness trickling down his throat. "Should I?"

The man sighed. "I see." A long-nailed finger tapped the glass case over the grinning black fox mask. "You made this?"

Rusty set his hand on the case. "The mask is not for sale."

The blond frowned. "That wasn't the question." He leaned back on his heels. His chin went up and his brows dropped, his eyes narrowing to hard copper slits. "Did you make this mask?"

Rusty folded his arms across his chest and lifted a brow. If the guy was trying to intimidate him, it wasn't going to work. "Yes. I did."

"Well, that explains everything." The man snorted and shook his head. "Clever."

Rusty scowled. "That explains what?"

He smiled. "May I see it?"

The hair rose on the back of Rusty's neck. He absolutely did not want this man handling his mask. "It's not for sale."

The blond guy chuckled, a soft, velvety, sensual sound. "I heard you the first time." He leaned close to Rusty. The scent of warm leather from his coat drifted from his body. Warm leather, incense and something…else. "What would you say if I told you that I have the same mask, in white?"

There was a rushing in Rusty's ears and he couldn't quite catch his breath. The guy was way too close. "What?" He unfolded his arms and took a step back. It took an entire breath to realize what the guy had just said. He stared. "You have a mask like mine?"

The young man's smile sharpened, and he eased back. "Exactly like it, in white."

Rusty felt a chill raise every hair on his body. That was impossible. The other guy's fox mask couldn't be like his.

The blond guy's dark brow lifted, and he licked his lips. "I'll show you mine, if you show me yours."

Warmth scalded Rusty's cheeks. He was hitting on him. He turned away. "I have to get back to work." He had to get out of the guy's unnerving presence.

"Running away? Don't tell me guys never flirt with you?"

Rusty stiffened. They did, occasionally, but none this blindingly good-looking. He turned back to the guy and delivered a tight smile. "Don't tell me you've never been turned down?"

The blond folded his arms and grinned. "Actually, I haven't."

Rusty rolled his eyes. *Hello, towering ego...* He set his hands on his hips. "Seriously, I have work to get back to. Was there something else you wanted?"

"Fine, be that way." The blond waved his hand in dismissal. "I'm here to pick up the Japanese costumes for the Oriental Playhouse. Two men's outfits, formal *wafukus,* one in black and one in white."

Rusty sucked in a breath. The order was done, except for the white robe sitting on his machine. He frowned. "I thought pickup was tomorrow?"

The man's brows shot up. "Tomorrow?"

"The order isn't done." Rusty shook his head. "I'm still working on the white *wafuku.*"

"Damn it, Helena must have given you the wrong date." He turned away and wiped a palm down his face. "I need them for tonight's performance."

Rusty's brows shot up in surprise. "You're an actor?" No wonder he was so…pretty.

"You could say that." The blond guy looked away and shrugged. "I am a professional entertainer." He looked over at Rusty. "So, how close are you to being finished?"

Rusty sucked on his bottom lip. "I should be finished in an hour."

"Excellent! Then I'll wait." The guy smiled. "You don't mind, do you?"

Rusty clenched his teeth. "And if I did?"

The blond leaned back against the glass counter, his smile broadening to show teeth with incisors just at trace longer than normal. "Pity I'm a paying customer, no?"

Rusty forced a smile on his face, showing his teeth. "There's a coffee shop right down the street. You could wait there."

The man's brow lifted and he leaned closer, looming over Rusty. "I think…not."

Rusty leaned away, gritting his teeth. "We don't have a place for waiting customers."

The blond tilted his head. "I'm sure you can find a spare chair somewhere for the customer that just doled out a couple thousand dollars for only two costumes."

Rusty glared at him. *What a prick!* He turned his back on him and strode for the basement door. "Fine, follow me."

The blond chuckled. "Don't mind if I do."

Rusty rolled his eyes. *What did I do to deserve this guy?* He opened the basement door, revealing the stairs. "Watch your step.

"One moment." The guy shoved in front of Rusty blindingly fast, jamming one hand against the doorframe, blocking the stairs.

"What…?" Startled, Rusty fell back against the doorframe, right by the young man's hand.

The blond guy leaned close and smiled from barely a kiss away. Bathed in sunlight from the skylight directly over the door, his hair was a fall of frost white framing the sculpted perfection of his face. "I'm Shiro."

*Shiro…* Rusty froze and stared. His heart hammered in his chest.

Warmth spread up his throat, into his cheeks and spilled downward, knotting low. His gaze was drawn to the curve of his full lips, so like the dream… He could almost feel the press of those lips against his, and the velvet caress of his tongue. He lifted his chin. Would they taste the same?

Shiro's lids dropped low over his copper eyes. His head tilted slightly and his lips parted. "Yes?"

Alarm shivered through Rusty and a sweat broke out across his lower back. *What…?* He slammed back against the doorframe and turned his face away. *Damn that wet dream.* It was messing with his head. And other parts of his anatomy. He eased to the side.

Shiro stepped in and set his other hand flat against the wall on other side of Rusty's body, framing him and blocking his escape. His smile broadened. "Aren't you forgetting something?"

*Huh?* Rusty stared up at him. The scent of warm leather rolled from the graceful young man's body, tinged with a vague hint of exotic incense and something else, something…feral, and familiar. He couldn't think past it. The blood pounded in his head too loudly, filling him with heat, filling him with…urgency. His jeans became uncomfortably tight. He tore his gaze away and scrambled for a coherent thought.

Shiro's brow lifted and his smile broadened. "Well?"

Rusty blinked. Was he supposed to say something? Desperate to fill the weighted silence, he said the first thing that popped into his head. "Isn't Shiro a Japanese name?" His voice came out a tad too tight. "You don't look Japanese." He winced, just a little. Why the hell had he said that? God, he couldn't think straight around this guy.

"Much of my family lives in Japan, but we're not Japanese." Shiro chuckled. "Though I do practice a few of their ancient arts." His gaze dropped to Rusty's mouth. "And you are…?"

Rusty's gaze was drawn to Shiro's parted lips. Visceral memory of the dream seared through him, of kissing that mouth, of feeling that mouth on his skin… His cock throbbed in his jeans, violently hard.

He gasped and turned sharply away. *Get your shit together and think, damn it!* What was it the guy wanted? Oh, yeah… "I'm Rusty."

"Rusty." Shiro spoke as though tasting the name on his lips and tongue. "I see." He leaned back, releasing Rusty, and smiled, showing his white teeth. "It goes with your red hair."

"My hair is brown." Rusty scowled and folded his arms over his chest, covering the signs of his erect nipples poking against the thin fabric of his turtleneck.

Shiro snorted. "Indoors it does look brown, almost black, but in sunlight, it's quite plain that your hair is a very dark auburn red." He smiled. "Hidden fire; I like that." He turned and started down the steps, his long gray coat sweeping behind him, leaving Rusty behind.

# ~ *Three* ~

"**H**IDDEN FIRE?" ANGER FLUSHED THROUGH RUSTY IN A NICE, REFRESHING wave. He tromped down the steps after Shiro. "What the hell is that supposed to mean?"

Shiro's soft chuckle drifted up the stairs. "What's the matter? Can't take a compliment?"

Rusty's shoulders tightened. "I can take anything you can dish out."

Shiro turned on the stairs, and smiled at Rusty "Is that an offer?"

"What...?" Rusty scowled and his heels thumped heavily on the stairs. He'd already said he wasn't interested. How clear did he have to make it? "Quit being a pain in my ass!"

"A pain in your ass?" Shiro's full lips curved up into a sly grin. "But we haven't even kissed yet."

Rusty stiffened. Heat flushed up his throat and into his face. "Quit pushing me, I mean it."

Shiro's eyes narrowed, but his smile remained. "If I'd intended to *push* you, you'd already be up against that wall."

Rusty stopped startled. *What...?* Anger seared through him. The prick was *trying* to piss him off! He stepped downward, glaring at Shiro. "Look, I don't care if you *are* a paying customer, cut it out. Or do you want a fist in the mouth that badly?"

Shiro turned away slightly and set his fingers over his smiling lips. "Oh, my, how violent."

Rusty's hands tightened into fists and his lip curled baring his teeth in a cold smile. "If you want to see violence..." His voice dropped into a low rumble. "I can show you violence." He slammed his right fist into the brick wall beside the stairs. The brick crunched like glass. He pulled his fist away from the wall, leaving a shallow fist-sized hole. Shards of brick and mortar fell, scattering down the stairs. Still smiling, Rusty blew the dust from his undamaged knuckles and waggled his fingers. "Do we have an understanding?"

Shiro's eyes widened and his brows lifted. "Impressive." He turned away, jamming his hands into his pants pockets. "You may consider your point made." He proceeded down the stairs to the bottom.

*Thank God...* Rusty took several deep breaths to gain control of his temper. He hadn't actually planned on hitting the brick wall quite that hard, but something about this guy really set his nerves on edge.

Shiro flipped his long silver tail over his shoulder and looked around the basement workshop with interest. "So this is where you work?"

Rusty took the last few steps down and slanted a guarded glance at Shiro. "Yeah."

Shiro walked around, peering at the various sketches hanging on the walls. "Is this where you made the mask?"

Rusty pulled out his chair by the old Singer machine. "No, I made that before they hired me, when I was still in high school." He dropped into the small chair and waved toward the other machines. "Feel free to grab a chair or stool from wherever." Determined to ignore the tall, blond annoyance, he gathered up the white silk and positioned it for the last bit of hemming, then set his foot on the pedal. The sewing machine hummed.

Shiro wandered about, poking into drawers and peering at pictures in silence. It was almost relaxing. Shiro abruptly knelt down by the bookcase in the far corner of the room. "Oh, are these sketchbooks? Is it all right if I look?"

Rusty shifted, the silk spilling into his lap. "Sure, look at whatever you like, just put it back when you're done."

"Yes, of course." Shiro selected a couple of large brown leather, ribbon-bound scrapbooks. He carried them to the large cutting table in the room's center and perched on a stool. Resting his chin on his fist, he slowly leafed through the pages.

Rusty ignored him to concentrate on dealing with the white silk. His mind drifted into calm order.

A full hour passed, marked by the sporadic humming of the machine and the whisper of turning pages.

Rusty snipped the last threads and drew the finished robe from the machine. "There we are."

Shiro looked up from the sketchbook he was studying. "You're done?" He rose from the stool and walked over. "May I see it?"

"Sure." Rusty stood up and shook out the robe, holding it by the shoulders to reveal the swirling blue and silver clouds sweeping up the back and along the trailing sleeves. "The *wafuku* design was a little odd. I've never heard of a robe with the skirt split in back."

"It was necessary for the part." Shiro frowned and brushed a finger down the design on the fabric. His eyes widened. He glanced at Rusty, then brushed his fingers down the fabric again. "Is that painted directly onto the silk?"

Rusty nodded. "I couldn't find anything with the right design, so I bought inks specifically for silk and handpainted the entire bolt. I had to do the same with the black silk."

Shiro's brows lifted. "You handpainted all of this?" He tilted his head and bit down on his bottom lip, staring at the design sweeping across the shimmering silk. "You're quite an artist."

"Thanks." Warmth crept into Rusty's cheeks and he dropped his gaze. It was nice to be appreciated.

Shiro looked up at him. "May I see the black *wafuku?*"

"Yeah, sure." Rusty stepped past Shiro, set the white robe carefully on the cutting table, then walked toward the back wall and the fabric-swathed clothing rack against it. "It's over here."

"You didn't have to paint the *wafukus.*" Shiro stepped closer. "I would have taken them in plain white and black silk."

Rusty tugged the white dustsheet back, revealing the crammed clothing rack. "I thought about it, but it just didn't feel right to leave them plain." He pulled a hanger free that held a long, dark robe draped in clear plastic.

"Do you always follow your feelings?" Shiro's voice was quiet, nearly a whisper.

"Following my instincts is easier than doing something over." Rusty pulled the plastic off, then tugged the painted midnight robe free, leaving the forest-green hakima, gold under-robe and the autumn-red *obi* on the hanger. "I've ruined more than one costume by not going with my feelings the first time around."

"Ruined them?"

"When stuff doesn't go right, I, um…" Rusty winced. "I lose my temper and end up ripping it apart." He spread the black robe across the cutting table. Green and red maple leaves covered the shimmering, rainbow-hued midnight silk. "I couldn't afford to do that with these. Silk is expensive as hell."

"Ah, yes, the artistic temperament." Shiro tilted his head and smiled. "Tempestuous."

Rusty's heart clenched. *That word…* He shook his head. *Forget it…*

Shiro leaned over the table. "Incredible…" He spread his hand out, his long nails brushing against the silk. "The detailing is superb." His silver hair spilled onto the black silk and autumn leaves.

Rusty couldn't look away from the fall of silver against the night dark silk covered in bright leaves. His heart pulsed hard. He winced and set his hand over his chest.

Shiro smiled. "You really put your heart and soul into this."

*Heart and soul…*

Rusty's heart slammed in his chest too hard, painfully hard. So hard he couldn't breathe past it. *It hurts…* His fingers dug into his chest. *It hurts!* The wind rushed in his ears. He groaned, but couldn't hear his own voice past the sound of the night wind rushing through the leaves.

His knees buckled. Like falling leaves across a night sky, he floated downward. The ground felt so warm, so peaceful, as though he lay under a hot scarlet blanket. Someone pressed painfully against his chest, talking—no, yelling—in his ear.

"Do you want to live?"

Did he want...what?

"I can save you, but it will cost you." Copper eyes in a beautiful, youthful face framed with silver hair stared into his. "Your heart and soul, will you give them to me?"

He gasped in a deep breath, and shuddered violently. His eyes opened. Rusty looked up into Shiro's mature face. He was sprawled across the floor with his head in Shiro's lap. *What the hell...?*

Shiro leaned over him and smiled. "Comfortable?"

Rusty shouted in shock and struggled to get out of Shiro's lap.

Shiro smile soured. "Am I that terrifying?"

"Why am I sitting on you?" He got himself upright with his butt firmly planted on the cement floor. His head spun and he rubbed at his chest in confusion. "What happened?"

"What happened?" Shiro leaned back against the drawers of the cutting table, his hands folded on his upraised knee, perfectly at ease on the floor. "You collapsed."

"No..." Rusty struggled up onto his feet. "I don't collapse." His legs shook under him, threatening to spill him back onto the floor.

Shiro snorted and rose to his feet. "Oh, really?" He caught Rusty by the elbow, keeping him upright. "Well, you certainly did an excellent imitation of a collapse."

Rusty scowled and pulled away, grabbing for the edge of the cutting table. "No, you don't understand." He stared at the black robe and his pulse pounded in his temples. "I don't just...collapse. I don't get sick, I don't get hurt, I don't even catch colds!" He wiped a palm down his face. "This kind of shit doesn't happen to me!"

"How hard have you been working?" Shiro set a warm hand on Rusty's shoulder and smiled just a little. "Perhaps you just need rest?"

Rusty frowned. Was that it? Was he just tired? Well, his sleep had been off for a while, and then he'd had that weird dream... He eased out from under the heat of Shiro's hand. "Maybe you're right. I probably just need some sleep."

Shiro pursed his lips and glanced from the corner of his eye. "You could be hungry. When was the last time you ate?"

"That can't be it." Rusty shook his head. "I'm always hungry." It didn't matter how much he ate, he could stuff himself stupid and he'd still be hungry. He snorted. "But I've never passed out from just hunger." He looked down at his slender body. And he never gained any weight, no matter how much food he packed in.

"People do pass out from hunger, you know. Tell you what..." Shiro folded his hands together and leaned close. "Why don't I take you out for a nice steak dinner, my treat? After we deliver the costumes to the playhouse, you can stay to see my performance. We'll take my car, so you won't have to drive." He leaned back and smiled. "Dinner and a show; what could be more relaxing?"

Rusty stared at him, wide-eyed. That sounded suspiciously like a date. "I don't know..."

Shiro brushed a palm against the black silk spread across the table. "Wouldn't you like to see your costumes as they were meant to be seen, on the stage?" He smiled and shrugged. "Of course, I'll be on stage wearing one of them, so you'll be sitting in the audience by yourself."

Rusty swept his hand across one of the leaves he'd painstakingly painted on the black silk. It didn't sound like too bad of an idea. He'd love to see how his costumes looked on the actors under stage lights and he'd be sitting in the audience, so he could leave at any time. He could just catch a taxi home. He'd at least get a free dinner out of it.

Shiro turned his back to the table and leaned against it. "Since I'll be wearing the white fox mask, you could bring yours and see how it compares."

Rusty jolted. He'd forgotten that Shiro was supposed to have a mask like his. How alike were they, really? He frowned and narrowed his eyes at Shiro. "How come you're being nice all of a sudden?"

Shiro turned to the side and looked down at the silk robe. He shrugged. "Consider it an apology for teasing you when you did such gorgeous work for me." He bit down on his bottom lip, but his sideways gaze held amusement. "I almost feel guilty."

Rusty stiffened. "Almost?"

Shiro flipped back his silver tail and grinned shamelessly. "Oh, come on!" He poked a finger at Rusty. "You're so dead serious about everything, how could I resist?" He lifted a brow. "You really should loosen up a little."

Rusty rolled his eyes and sighed. "Fine, whatever..."

"Excellent!" Shiro grinned and threw out his arms. "I know a nice little Irish pub that serves wonderful steaks and decent beer."

Rusty shook his head and smiled in spite of himself. "I'll take the steak, but you can keep the beer." He tugged at his collar. "But, I'll need to go home and change out of my shirt first." The black turtleneck was seriously itching.

Shiro leaned back against the cutting table and folded his arms. "Isn't this a costume shop? Why not pull something off the rack?" He tapped his bottom lip with a long-nailed finger. "Something with full sleeves and maybe a vest?" He grinned. "You are going to a play, after all."

Rusty rolled his eyes. "I'll see what I can find." He jabbed a finger toward Shiro. "You stay down here!"

Shiro folded his arms across his chest and smiled. "You're sure you don't want any assistance?"

"No, thank you." Rusty snorted. "I really don't think the walls could take it." He jabbed a thumb over his shoulder, indicating the hole he'd punched in the brick wall.

Shiro covered his mouth with his hand, but did a poor job of hiding his broad grin. "You may be right."

With Shiro's assistance, it only took a few minutes to wrap both costumes in clear plastic for traveling and then Rusty went upstairs to find something to wear.

It wasn't difficult to find a fairly nice full-sleeved, pirate-shirt in black silk and a midnight green damask waistcoat. The shirt and vest didn't even look bad with his black jeans. Unfortunately, the bandage on his throat was soaked through. His scars were still seeping blood. In the upstairs restroom, he replaced his bandage and wound a black silk and lace cravat around the shirt's collar to hide it.

# ~ _four_ ~

*I*N HIS BULKY BLACK WOOL WINTER COAT, HIS ARMS FULL OF SILK WRAPPED IN protective plastic, Rusty led Shiro up the stairs to the main showroom. He set the costumes on the glass counter and nodded to Des, standing behind the register. "I'm going to deliver the Playhouse order." He unlocked the glass case and pulled out the grinning black fox mask. "Can you lock up the store for me?" He shoved the mask into his knapsack and zipped it closed.

Des glanced at Shiro, then smiled uneasily at Rusty. "Yeah, no problem. Be careful, okay?"

Rusty frowned. *Be careful?* That was an odd thing for her to say. Des was one of the few people well aware of Rusty's unusual—and unpredictable—strength. "Yeah, sure."

Shiro smiled at Des. "I will take very good care of him."

Des's eyes widened behind her glasses. She pasted on a huge, fake smile and gripped her long, dark braid. "Uh, sure, okay. Have a good night."

"Good night, Des." Rusty nudged Shiro with his elbow. "Ready?"

Shiro nodded and headed for the front door. At his heels, Rusty looked back at Des. She stared after him, her hands clenched around her braid.

Rusty made a fist and nodded toward Shiro's retreating back, indicating that he'd knock some sense into him if things got out of hand.

Des smile kicked up a notch, and she nodded.

Out in the back parking lot under the winter bare trees, Shiro

22

opened the trunk of a cream and gold Jaguar.

Rusty stilled. "You drive a Jag?" Good God, how much money did this actor make? Was he in the movies or something?

Shiro smiled and took the plastic-wrapped silk from Rusty's arms. "Yes, I drive a Jag, among other things." He set the costumes in the empty trunk. "They'll be safe there." He closed the trunk and walked around to open the passenger door. He leaned over the window frame, obviously waiting for Rusty to get in. "Ready for some steak? I'm starved!"

Rusty's jaw tightened. Holding the door open was something you did for a girl, or a date. "I am not a girl. Don't treat me like one."

Shiro rolled his eyes and his smile tightened. "I am well aware that you are not a girl." He abandoned Rusty's door to walk around to the driver's side. "I was being polite."

Rusty shot Shiro a glare over the roof of the Jag. *Polite, my ass...* He got in, closing the door behind him, and set his knapsack by his feet. *I am definitely going home in a taxi before the play ends.* After he saw what his costumes looked like onstage. After he saw just how closely his mask matched Shiro's.

Shiro wove through the late-afternoon city traffic with deft skill and a dash of smiling recklessness while keeping up a steady stream of chatter on nothing in particular. His comments ranged from the city's winter weather to the mental capacity of the other drivers on the road.

In spite of himself, Rusty began adding to Shiro's bitingly sarcastic observations, and even laughed on occasion.

In less time than Rusty expected, Shiro pulled into a tiny back street behind a row of renovated warehouses, then parked in a postage-stamp-sized parking lot along the two-story stone wall that bordered the historic district.

Rusty got out of the car, leaving his knapsack on the seat, and closed the door. He stared up at the aged brick wall dividing the present from the past and shivered for no apparent reason whatsoever.

"This way, Rusty!"

Rusty turned his back on the wall and followed Shiro across the parking lot to a narrow wooden door painted bright green. A broad sign over the door announced that they were entering 'Fiddlers' Green Pub'.

Done in the Victorian style, the three story plaster-walled restaurant was crammed with antique furniture, dusty knickknacks and yellowed paintings in battered frames. A massive bar, supposedly imported piece-by-piece straight from Dublin, Ireland, took up the full length of the long right-hand wall on the ground floor.

A cute hostess led them up the polished staircase to the next floor. Just past a collection of cloth-covered tables, deep shadows filled candle-lit nooks along the wall. Only a small handful of patrons occupied a few of the tables. The hostess placed the menus on a table in an isolated corner and left. In mere seconds, an even cuter waitress appeared.

Shiro practically tore his gray leather coat off and sat. He had the menu open before Rusty could get his black wool coat unbuttoned.

Rusty smiled and set his coat over the back of the empty chair by the wall. "I guess you weren't kidding about being hungry."

Shiro's narrowed gaze lifted over the top edge of the menu and focused on Rusty. His smile turned sharp. "You have no idea." He turned to the hovering waitress and ordered the ribeye. "As rare as you can serve it."

That sounded good to Rusty, so he ordered the same.

Shiro leaned back on his chair and smiled, his copper eyes gleaming in the candlelight. "I like that black shirt, cravat and vest ensemble; very neo-romantic. It suits you."

Rusty's cheeks warmed. He dodged Shiro's heavy-lidded stare. "Um, thanks."

Shiro tapped the table with a long nail. "So how did you get into costuming?"

Rusty shifted in his seat. "My art teacher. He liked the way I did the fox mask, so he sent me to the costume shop. The owner is a friend of his. Turned out that I had a real knack for costuming." He smiled sourly. "Now, I'm a manager."

Shiro's brow lifted. "You've done nothing else?"

Rusty shrugged. "There was nothing else I liked doing."

"What about college?"

Rusty dropped his gaze. He'd wanted to go to University, but after the accident, his life had gotten seriously messed up. The nightmares, the sudden increase in physical strength causing him to drop out of sports or risk seriously hurting someone, his parent's divorce… Life had sucked big time, and his grades had suffered too much to make a university scholarship. "I took some costuming courses."

The waitress came back and set a glass of water before Rusty, then put a glass of dark beer in front of each of them. "Your order will be out shortly."

Rusty eyed the beer with grave misgivings. "I didn't order that."

Shiro lifted his glass. "I did. You said you needed to relax."

"Thanks, but…" Rusty looked away. "I don't drink."

"At all?"

Rusty winced. "No tolerance." *At all.*

Shiro smiled. "It's just one beer."

Rusty sighed. Yes, it was just one beer, and if he drank it he wouldn't be able to stand. As physically strong as he was, even a small amount of alcohol knocked him flat on his ass. He smiled at Shiro. "I was never much of a party animal."

Shiro shrugged. "Suit yourself." He took a healthy swallow from his glass, and proceeded to grill Rusty about his experiences as a costumer.

Rusty smiled and replied. It was rather nice to find someone so interested in his work.

The steak arrived and conversation drifted into historic theater. Shiro had a passion for antique plays. Rusty hid his smiles behind his napkin. Considering that Shiro was so handsome—practically beautiful—the ornate historic costumes would seriously set off his incredible looks.

A particularly spicy bite from the side dish made Rusty grab for his glass. He had a full swallow of beer down before he realized what he was drinking. He set the glass down hard. "Ah, shit…" He grabbed for his water glass, but it was empty; he'd already finished it.

Shiro's brows rose. "Rusty?"

Rusty rose from the table. "I'll be right back." He needed to get some water in his stomach to dilute the beer. He did not need to be drunk in Shiro's company. He took a step away from the table and his head swam. He was forced to sit back down.

Shiro stared at his plate and cut a piece of steak. "Is something wrong?"

Rusty looked over at Shiro. "What kind of beer was that?"

"Belgian." Shiro smiled. "A little strong for you?"

Rusty gripped the table. As long as he stayed still, his head was fine. "You could say that."

"Really?" Shiro shrugged. "The alcohol content is a little high in Belgian beer, but you only had one swallow."

Rusty winced. Shiro was making him sound like a pansy. He picked up his fork. Maybe the food would help. "It's nothing."

Shiro smiled. "Good!" He turned his wrist to look at his silver wristwatch. "Oh, damn, the time. We need to hurry, so eat up."

Rusty cleared his plate while Shiro signed the bill for the waitress. Shiro rose to his feet and picked up his long leather coat. "Ready?"

"Sure." Rusty rose to put on his coat and couldn't quite get his arms into his sleeves.

Shiro slid into his coat and rolled his eyes. "Let me help you with that." He got Rusty into his coat, then sat on the edge of the bench to button it. "Good lord, you weren't kidding about not being able to handle alcohol."

Rusty scowled and gripped the edge of the table, teetering on his feet while Shiro finished buttoning his coat. "I'm fine." *As long as I hold still.* He looked across the table-crammed room and eyed the staircase leading to the lower floor. He swallowed.

Shiro got up and stepped out of the booth. "You okay to walk by yourself?"

Rusty faced the staircase. "Sure." All he had to do was walk in a straight line...through all those tables. He took a step and rocked into the chair by the closest table. He grabbed for it, but the chair slipped through his fingers and clattered to the floor. Overbalancing, he teetered after it.

Shiro caught Rusty's arm, steadying him back on his feet, and grinned. "Liar."

Rusty grabbed onto Shiro's arm. "Fine, you gave me the beer, you can get me out of here." Not that he had much of a choice.

Shiro smiled. "My pleasure." He looped his arm through Rusty's.

"That's what I'm afraid of." Rusty winced. He hadn't meant to say that out loud.

Shiro snorted and urged Rusty forward. "Relax, I prefer my men sober."

Rusty frowned at him, unsure if that was a comforting thought or not.

Shiro's steady hand under his elbow got Rusty safely through all the tables. At the top of the stairs, Shiro set his arm firmly around Rusty's waist. "Easy now, one step at a time..."

Rusty grabbed onto the handrail and proceeded downward. Held tight against Shiro's strong, muscular body and inundated by the taller man's exotic scent, Rusty's heart began to pound. Sweat formed and dripped from his brow. It took forever to reach the bottom.

Downstairs, Shiro kept his arm around Rusty's waist to navigate their way through the tables on their way to the door.

The outside chill was a welcome relief.

Shiro guided Rusty to the car and opened the passenger door.

Rusty dropped heavily into the seat. Safe at last...

Shiro ducked his head to peer in at Rusty. "What? No complaints about me holding the door this time?"

Rusty grabbed for the door handle. "Oh, shut up!" He tugged it closed.

Shiro laughed and walked around the car to get in on the driver's side. "Now then, on to the playhouse!" He started the car and in a matter of minutes, he drove them through the massive wooden gates marking the historic district. Several winding and frighteningly narrow back streets later, they approached a second and older gate arching over the road.

Rusty stared up at the huge red gate. "Isn't this the old red light district?"

Shiro lifted his chin, dodging his gaze, and swept his fingers through his long silvery tail. "The playhouse is in the historic courtesan quarter, yes."

Rusty frowned at him startled. The modern sex shops, strip joints and gambling parlors had long since moved to another whole part of the city, but the courtesan quarter was still known for adult entertainments—of the exotic and expensive kind.

Was Shiro a…male escort? He jerked his gaze away. It was none of his business. Escort or not, who was he to judge what other people did for a living? "I…see."

"I perform in adult versions of historic plays." Shiro's voice was very cool.

*Adult plays?* Shiro was taking him to see an adult play? *Uh-oh…* Rusty swallowed hard. "Sounds… interesting."

Shiro smiled. "Scared?"

Rusty scowled. "Of what? A play?"

Shiro chuckled and pulled onto a narrow drive that led into a hidden parking lot jammed between several old buildings. "Can you walk?"

"Watch me." Rusty opened the door and got out. He was going to walk on his own if it killed him.

# ~ *five* ~

WITH THE PLASTIC-WRAPPED SILK COSTUMES DRAPED OVER ONE ARM AND his knapsack over his opposite shoulder, Rusty stood at the bottom of the short staircase, staring up at the narrow black double doors that waited under the sweeping, shingled roof of the antique Oriental Playhouse. A chill winter breeze ruffled the dark hair falling across his brow and raised the small hairs on the back of his neck.

He was going to see an adult play with a man that was clearly interested in him. How had he let himself get talked into this?

He looked up the narrow alley that served as a street. Above the peaked and shingled rooftops, the last of the sunlight gave way to the deep blue of twilight and stars. Just two turns away the district was crammed with people, but here? The lights were off, the doors were unmarked and no one was there. It was like…a ghost town.

Shiro started up the steps and looked over his shoulder. "Do you need help?"

Heat rushed into Rusty's cheeks. "I walked this far, didn't I?" Two whole blocks in the chill shadows of utterly dark shops.

Shiro smiled. "I guess the alcohol has finally worn off?"

Rusty tightened his grip on the silk. "Looks that way." He wiped his other palm down his black jeans and started up the steps behind Shiro. He was out of his freaking mind.

Shiro pulled the cord by the door and a bell sounded inside.

The lights over the playhouse door blinked on and the right door opened. A handsome older woman in a neat, dark suit stepped out. Her dark hair was drawn up into an extravagant knot festooned with glittering pins. She smiled with bright red lips. "Master Shiro.

Welcome back."

Shiro tilted his head toward Rusty. "This is Rusty, from the costume shop."

The woman smiled. "Hello, Rusty, I'm Helena. Welcome!" She stepped back through the door, holding it open for him.

Rusty nodded politely to Helena, and followed Shiro past her, stepping across the threshold and into shadow. A hard shiver traveled up his spine.

"Your room is ready." Helena closed the door behind them and pulled a pair of plastic flip-flops and a pair of embroidered black satin slippers from a shelved cupboard built into the wall right behind the door. She offered the slippers to Shiro and held the flip-flops out to Rusty. "I'll take your shoes."

Rusty blinked. "My…shoes?"

Shiro traded his dress shoes for the slippers and snorted in clear amusement. "This is a Japanese establishment. You don't wear shoes inside."

"Oh…" Rusty leaned over and tugged his shoes off, replacing them with the oversized flip-flops.

"Thank you, Helena. This way, Rusty." Shiro led Rusty at a swift pace through a cedar-walled and deeply shadowed maze of tiny dimly-lit hallways with low ceilings. Everything was so damned dark. Rusty could make out that there was a carpet on the floor, but had no clue as to what color it was.

Helena walked quietly at their heels.

Shiro stopped at a sliding door and turned. "Thank you, Helena, that will be all." He shoved the door wide and pushed Rusty toward it. "I'll send Rusty through the small stage door before I go on."

Helena pouted and crossed her arms. "I could seat him now and he could see the entire play."

Shiro's smile tightened. "He's a personal guest."

Helena's eyes widened. She darted a look at Rusty. "He's one of…?"

Shiro waved a hand, cutting her off. "More like a foundling."

Rusty had no clue what the hell they were talking about.

"Of course." Helena bowed her head, dropping her gaze, and backed away. "I will leave you to your...pleasures." She turned and hurried away down the hall.

Rusty frowned after her. *Pleasures?*

Shiro's hand closed around his upper arm. "Go on in." He pushed.

Rusty tipped backwards, nearly falling through the wall opening. "Hey!"

Shiro stepped in after him and slid the door closed sharply, right in front of Rusty's nose. "My apologies, but I'm in something of a hurry." Shiro flashed a smile and stepped past Rusty.

"What...?" Rusty turned around and faced an enormous windowless room. The wooden walls were completely bare. A huge, thick rug in red and gold commanded the center of the room, with a scrollwork Victorian chaise longue upholstered in wine velvet along the carpet's back edge. A battered suitcase had been shoved beneath it. A very plain folding paper wall screen blocked off the room's far right corner.

On the right edge of the carpet, a massive trunk stood on end, and open, overflowing with ornate silks. On the left edge of the carpet was an ornate full-length mirror positioned by a decorative table, covered in theater make-up, with a matching chair.

A low and somewhat shabby table in the carpet's center held a plain black tea service for two. The light came from an off-white ball-shaped paper lantern that hung poised at the center of the ceiling, tinting the entire room and everything in it a little yellow.

There was something wrong with this picture, but Rusty couldn't quite put his finger on what it was. It just seemed...off. "Shiro...?"

Shiro peeled out of his coat and strode for the chaise longue. "Go ahead and take off your coat." He tossed his coat over the back of the longue. "You can set the costumes over there." He pointed at the overflowing trunk on the right.

"Oh..." Rusty shook his head and strode for the trunk. "Sure, fine, whatever…" He set the plastic-wrapped silk on the top of the trunk and shrugged out of the heavy black wool coat. There really wasn't a reason to keep it on. The building was over-warm and he'd already started to sweat.

Shiro took the coat from Rusty's hand and tossed over the back of the longue. "Would you mind unwrapping my costume?" With his back to Rusty, Shiro pulled up his gray sweater, revealing a milk-pale but finely muscled back. He dropped the sweater over the end of the longue and reached for the waistband of his slacks. His buckle jangled, indicating the belt's release.

Rusty jerked his gaze away and tore the plastic from the white costume, just to give his hands something to do—and his eyes something to look at other than the slender man stripping right behind him. He separated the shimmering *wafuku* from the white under-robe. "How did I get roped into helping you dress?"

"Logic, actually. You made the costume, you'd know best how to wear it."

"Great." Rusty shoved the pale gray trousers toward Shiro without looking. "Here."

"You have a problem with nudity?" Shiro's deep voice held amusement.

Rusty stiffened. "I have a problem with someone pushing the point when he knows damned well I'm not interested."

Shiro took the trousers from his hand and chuckled. Fabric rustled. "I'm not so sure about that."

Rusty held out the snowy under-robe. "Not so sure about what?"

Shiro took the robe and fabric rustled. He leaned close to Rusty's ear. "I'm not so sure about you not being interested."

Rusty turned to glare at him. "Would my fist…?" He stopped, the words crashing to a halt on his tongue. "Uh…"

Shiro stood only inches away wearing only the full-sleeved and floor-length white under robe. His silver hair flowed free over his broad shoulders and down his back in a frost-white swathe to his narrow hips, matching the robe's snowy whiteness perfectly. Held closed by small ties on either side, the robe was open from neck to waist, revealing Shiro's fairly muscular chest.

Beneath it, he was completely nude. The pale gray pants had been draped over the back of the chaise longue. Shiro smiled. "I'm dressed. Feel better?"

*Feel better?* Rusty's heart beat in his throat. *Not really.* He'd never seen a man that freaking handsome, not even in magazines. Heat flushed up his throat and into his cheeks. He swallowed. "You're not wearing the pants?" His voice came out only a tad tight.

"No." Shiro's smile sharpened. "They'll only get in the way."

Rusty blinked. *Get in the way?* He decided right there and then he really didn't want to think about it.

Shiro turned his back to Rusty, presenting the split back of the under-robe and a view of his muscular calves and thighs. "You're going to have to help me with the *wafuku* and the *obi.* I'm not going to be able to knot the sash properly with those long sleeves."

Rusty could not stop staring at the fabric hugging the perfect curve of Shiro's muscular rump.

Shiro looked over his shoulder and raised his brow. "Rusty, the *wafuku?*"

Rusty jerked his gaze from Shiro's backside. "Uh, sure…" He turned sharply around to collect the heavy white formal robe. Why was someone with a body like that and a face that belonged in Renaissance paintings interested in someone like him? He snorted. *No accounting for taste…*

He unfolded the heavy silk and lifted it, helping Shiro get his arms into the overlong sleeves of the robe. He tugged the under-robe sleeves into place and frowned at the overlapping split in the back. "You never did tell me why you wanted the back skirting split. It's not traditional."

Shiro folded the robe across his chest and chuckled. "You'll see."

Rusty turned to collect the broad, pale blue sash and unfolded the rich silk. "Is it some kind of secret?"

Shiro turned to face Rusty, holding the heavy silk robe closed with his right hand. "Something like that."

"Huh…" Rusty walked over with the sash held out in both hands. Unlike some *obis*, this type of sash had to be wrapped twice around the waist, then knotted in the front…

Shiro caught Rusty by the shoulders and shoved.

"What…?" Rusty fell backwards, and sprawled onto the longue. "Hey…!" One of his flip-flops came off his foot and tumbled to the floor. He jerked upright on the cushions. "What're you doing?"

Shiro smiled. "If you're sitting, it'll be easier to tie the *obi*."

Rusty blinked. Well, sitting would be easier than kneeling. "Oh, right." He held up the sash.

"Spread your legs, so I can get close enough." Shiro bit down on his bottom lip, clearly trying to bite back a smile. "Unless you'd rather I spread mine?"

Rusty stared up at Shiro. Shiro was naked under that robe with not a damned thing holding the white *wafuku* together but his hand and the two tiny bows on the sides to keep the under-robe closed. If he spread his legs, the robe would part and… "No, I'll do it!" Rusty jerked his knees wide.

Shiro's brow lifted. "Very well." He stepped between Rusty's spread thighs until his knees pressed against the edge of the Victorian longue.

Rusty stared straight at Shiro's belly, refusing to acknowledge the bulge in the silk only a hand-span below his chin. *Maybe this wasn't such a bright idea.* He sighed and leaned forward. *Too late now.* He reached around Shiro's waist and wound the sash, smoothing the silk to lay flat. Shiro's body was nearly hot under his palms. He couldn't believe how much heat Shiro's body gave off. And he smelled good…like forest, and night. And sex.

Shiro sighed. "You're good at this."

Rusty couldn't get a word out of his mouth. His heart was beating in it. And his jeans were getting way too tight. Damn it, he was getting hard again. He closed his eyes and tried to think calm thoughts, but his dick was not listening. *Fuck it.* He opened his eyes and formed the decorative knot in the center of the sash. He set his hands down. "There, you're done."

Shiro tilted his head. "Not quite." He leaned over Rusty and clasped the back of the couch with his left hand, his silver mane slipping forward and down his arm. "Kiss me."

"What?" Rusty looked up startled, then jerked back away from Shiro, but there was no place to go. "Hey!" He slammed a hand up against Shiro's chest. "What do you think you're doing?"

Shiro smiled. "Do you want to see my mask, the one that looks so much like yours?"

Rusty swallowed hard. Shiro's body was hot and solid against his palm. He could even feel his heart beating all the way through the layers of silk. "What has the mask got to do with...this?"

"Do you want to see it?" Shiro leaned against Rusty's palm and his brow lifted. "Yes or no?"

Rusty frowned up at him. He'd come all this way to see that damned mask. "Yes."

Shiro's smile sharpened into something feral, almost angry. He pressed harder against Rusty's palm. "Then kiss me."

"Damn it!" Rusty scowled. He didn't want to push against Shiro's chest any harder. Shiro was being a pain in the ass, but was so damned slender, Rusty might break a bone with his weird strength. "You really want to kiss me that bad?"

"I..." Shiro's smile dissolved, and he bit down on his bottom lip. "Yes."

Rusty stared. Good God, Shiro was serious. In fact, he looked almost...anxious. Rusty licked his lips. It was only a kiss, and he was physically strong enough to stop him if things got out of hand. He was physically strong enough to *break* him if things got out of hand. He sighed. "Fine, you can have a kiss."

# ~ Six ~

SITTING ON THE VICTORIAN CHAISE LONGUE, RUSTY STARED UP INTO SHIRO'S wide copper gaze, somewhat shocked. He'd just given a guy permission to kiss him. Sure the guy was gorgeous, and helping him get dressed had made him hard as a rock in his jeans, but still...

Shiro's brows lifted. "Rusty, remove your hand."

Rusty started. His palm was pressed against Shiro's chest, literally keeping him at arm's length. His heart felt like it was trying to pound its way out of his chest. He trembled, just a little. "I, uh..."

Shiro smiled. It wasn't exactly a comforting smile, not the way he was looming over Rusty while standing between his spread thighs. "Rusty, I'm not going to hurt you. It's just a kiss."

Rusty bit down on his bottom lip. He'd agreed to a kiss, and now he had to go through with it. *Damn it.* He eased his hand back from Shiro's chest, not sure what he should do with it.

Shiro twitched his robes to one side and raised a very naked knee. He set it on the cushion between Rusty's spread thighs, then reached out to set his right hand on Rusty's shoulder.

Rusty stiffened and very nearly yelped.

"Rusty?"

Rusty looked up. "Huh?"

Shiro descended, his lips brushing against Rusty's, delivering warmth and gentle softness.

Rusty blinked in surprise. *This...this isn't so bad.* Breath and an inquisitive tongue swept across Rusty's bottom lip. Rusty opened his mouth out of sheer force of habit. The tongue entered to caress him, carrying the slight zing of beer and something else; something wilder, and hauntingly familiar.

The hair rose on his neck. He knew those lips, he knew that tongue, he knew that odd, feral flavor…he knew this kiss. Heat stabbed down his spine to throb in his dick. He moaned and reached up to grasp the back of Shiro's neck, pulling him tighter against his mouth. He wrapped his arm around Shiro's waist, pulling him against his body, sucking on his tongue, sucking him in…

A slight shove against Rusty's shoulder tipped him to the side, knocking his other shoe off. His knee came up and he sprawled back against the cushions, one knee jammed against the back of the longue, his other foot still on the floor with Shiro's hot weight pressing down on top of him, chest to chest, belly to belly and between his spread thighs. Urgency seared through him. He pressed his hips upward, rubbing his aching cock against Shiro's hot belly.

Shiro moaned in reply, then his hands closed on Rusty's shoulders. He pushed, rising up and breaking the kiss. "You must have put everything into that mask. You taste almost pure human."

Rusty blinked up at him, staring into copper eyes that possessed slitted up-down pupils, not round ones, like a human. *What…?*

A pair of snow-white pointed ears parted the long silver hair that spilled loosely down his shoulders, cascading to the floor. Rising from the split back of his robes was an enormous bushy white fox tail waving slightly behind him, moving with the fluidity of flesh and blood. He smiled, showing over-long incisors. "Now do I look familiar?"

*Ears and a tail…?* And really big teeth.

Every hair on Rusty's body rose. The echoes of a forgotten nightmare pressed at the edges of his mind. He shouted in alarm and shoved upright. "What the fuck…?"

Shiro sat up wincing, his ears flicking back in clear annoyance. "Still so very short-tempered. You haven't changed a bit, Rusty…or should I say, Russell?"

Rusty froze. "What?" No one had called him by that name since high school. His neck throbbed, and wetness slithered down. "How did you know?"

"It's the name you gave me when we first met. I've been searching for you ever since." Shiro stared at Rusty, his smile gone and his cinnamon eyes hard. "We made a pact, you and I; a pact that you have yet to fulfill."

"What pact?" Rusty eased back on his elbows, leaning away, his gaze darting between Shiro's tall triangular ears and the fluffy white tail. "What the hell are you?"

"I'm a Kitsune, a fox spirit." Shiro's ears flicked forward and his smile shifted to hide his long teeth. "You'd think the ears and tail would give that away."

Rusty froze. He'd heard of fox spirits, but that was all fairy-tales, and make-believe... "This can't be real."

"Oh, I am very real." Shiro pressed a long-nailed finger against Rusty's vest. "And it's past time you lived up to your half of the bargain."

Rusty's mouth went dry. "Bargain?"

"Your heart and soul belongs to me. I already have your soul." Shiro pressed his palm against his chest, then rolled his eyes. "It's the rest of you I'm having trouble hanging on to." He smiled sourly. "Truthfully, I wasn't quite sure it was you, at first." He caught Rusty's chin and tilted Rusty's head to the side, focusing on his throat. "You're so weak, you feel nearly human. I barely recognized you."

"Nearly human?" Rusty stiffened and jerked his chin away. "I *am* human! I'm just a normal guy!"

Shiro snorted. One pointed fox ear tipped back briefly. "You're not a normal guy. You haven't been human since the autumn I saved your life."

Rusty swallowed. "You...what?"

Shiro smiled sourly and set his hand on his hip. "You still don't remember?"

"I have no clue what you're talking about!"

Shiro raised his chin and sniffed. "Your mind may not remember me, but your body clearly does." His gaze focused on Rusty's throat.

"You're bleeding from my bite. I've been smelling it since the moment I met you."

*His* bite? Rusty pressed his hand against his burning neck. His palm came away wet. He stared at the scarlet streaking his fingers.

Shiro came up on his knees, arching over Rusty. "Your body is offering me blood because you're hungry. In fact, you're very close to starvation."

Rusty simply could not believe what he was hearing. "My body is doing what?"

Shiro smiled but his gaze was narrow and hot. "Your body is begging me to feed you." His hands closed on Rusty's shoulders, scorching hot through the fabric, and powerful. "To maintain a physical form in this world, I need living blood. To maintain life in your body, you need a living spirit." He brushed his lips against Rusty's cheek. "Because you don't have one; I have it."

Rusty tried to wrap his brain around what Shiro was saying, but none of it sounded real. "You have...what?"

"Your soul." Shiro nuzzled under Rusty's ear, along the edges of the cravat. "You've been drinking from the souls of others to make up for your lack."

"No!" Panicked, Rusty shoved at Shiro with both hands. "I don't! I don't do that!"

Shiro grabbed Rusty's wrists, jerking them up over his head, and shoved, pushing Rusty back down onto the cushions. "Yes, you do." He caught Rusty's chin in his hand and leaned over him, his slitted copper gaze staring hard at him. "You have been for years." His long white hair fell past his shoulders, enveloping them both in a frosty curtain. "It's how you've managed to remain alive."

"This is bullshit! Let go!" Rusty jerked at his wrists and twisted, but couldn't pull free. For the first time, in a very long time, he wasn't strong enough. He gasped, shocked.

Shiro smiled, showing his fangs. "Yes, you are very strong, inhumanly strong, but then, so am I." His eyes narrowed and his ears flicked back to lie against his skull. "Do we have an understanding?"

Rusty couldn't escape the hands that held him, or the copper eyes staring into his. "Are you going to kill me?"

"Kill you?" Shiro snorted in disgust, and his ears turned up and to the sides. "No, idiot, I'm trying to save you." He released Rusty's hands and sat up. "I'm just glad I found you in time."

"Save me?" Rusty pushed up onto his elbows and scowled. "Save me from what? I was fine until you showed up!"

"You are anything but fine." Shiro opened his palm against Rusty's chest and shoved, pushing him back down without even trying.

"There's nothing wrong with me!" Rusty shoved at Shiro's hand, but couldn't move it from over his heart.

Shiro smiled sadly. "Rusty, you should not be this weak."

"Weak?" Rusty stared up at him. "I break damned near everything I touch!"

"Because you don't have enough power to control what strength you do have." Shiro shook his head and sighed. "It's a wonder you've managed to survive this long."

Rusty scowled. "I told you, I'm fine, thank you very much!"

"You are not fine." Shiro set his other palm against Rusty's chilled cheek. "Feeding through your costumes is a very clever way to live on the scraps from human passion, but it's not enough to maintain you. You are starving to death."

*My costumes?* Rusty's blood went cold. "What has this got to do with my costumes?"

"You're bleeding a little from the soul of everyone that wears anything you make. I could feel the spell the moment I touched the silk."

"I am not!" Rusty shook his head, pulling away from the palm against his cheek. "I don't do magic!"

Shiro rolled his eyes. "Rusty, you *are* magic. It's what you're made of." His ears flicked back. "Haven't you been listening?"

"Listening to what? What you're saying is insane!"

Shiro snorted. "No one does denial like a human." He leaned on his palm, pinning Rusty under him. "Think, Rusty. What do you do when a costume you've painstakingly created is returned?"

Rusty blinked. "It goes to the cleaners."

"It goes downstairs to your workroom, your den, and then what do you do with it?"

Rusty could feel something being drawn from him, something he didn't want to say, something he didn't want to know. He closed his eyes and shook his head. "I send it to the cleaners."

Shiro cupped Rusty's chin. "Look at me."

"No!" Rusty closed his eyes tighter and grabbed for Shiro's wrist, but it was like trying to bend steel. His groan sounded suspiciously like a whimper.

"Look at me!"

Rusty's eyes snapped open.

Shiro's copper gaze bored into his. "Rusty, what do you do with a costume on its return, before you send it to the cleaners?"

Rusty struggled, but he couldn't break Shiro's hold, or break from the hot copper gaze boring into his. "Shiro, please...!"

"Rusty..." Shiro's ears flicked back, laying flat. Flames seemed to dance in the slitted heart of his gaze. "Answer the question. What do you do with the costume before you send it to the cleaners? Say it."

"I..." He could not stop his mouth from answering. "I lay it out on the cutting table."

Shiro's brow rose and a smile lifted the corner of his mouth, exposing an overlong incisor. "And then you...?" His finger's tightened on Rusty's jaw. "Say it."

Rusty winced and clenched his jaw, but couldn't stop his lips from replying. "I...sleep on it."

Shiro nodded slowly and his tall ears eased forward. "Yes, you sleep on the costume, draining it of the life-force infused into the fabric."

"I..." Rusty trembled under him. *I don't!* He wanted to scream it, but the words wouldn't pass his lips. Because he did, every single time. He'd fall asleep, perched on a stool at the cutting table, clutching every costume he'd ever made. He'd awaken with the dawn with his face pressed into the fabric. "You're saying I'm a vampire?"

"I'm saying that your body is missing its spirit, so it feeds on the spirits of others. You've found an interesting way to do it without killing anyone, but if you keep on as you have been, sooner or later, the people that wear your costumes will begin to die."

Rusty shivered hard. "Die?"

"Yes." Shiro unknotted the cravat around Rusty's throat. "You'll do it just to survive. You won't be able to stop yourself." He pulled the blood-soaked cravat free. His fingers slid down to tug at the buttons of Rusty's vest, opening it, then began opening Rusty's shirt.

"Wait!" Rusty grabbed for Shiro's wrists. "What are you doing?"

"If I drink from you, your body will stop bleeding." Shiro eased his wrists free from Rusty's hands. "Don't worry, I won't take much." He jerked the bandage from Rusty's throat.

Rusty flinched, and hot wetness flowed down to his shoulder. "Shit."

Shiro bent over Rusty, his silk robes and long hair sweeping across Rusty's body.

Rusty grabbed for Shiro's shoulders, knowing damned well he couldn't do a thing to stop him.

"Relax." Shiro's voice purred directly against Rusty's ear. "You're acting like a frightened virgin."

Rusty scowled up into Shiro's inhuman eyes. "How else am I supposed to act when you're acting like a lust-crazed pervert?"

Shiro chuckled and turned Rusty's face to the side, exposing the full length of his throat. "Who's acting?"

Rusty shivered. "Was that supposed to make me feel better?"

"Quit whining and take it like a man." Shiro's open mouth pressed against Rusty's throat. His tongue laved against the seeping scars.

# ~ Seven ~

HOT, WET VELVET STROKED DOWN THE LONG MUSCLES ALONG THE SIDE OF Rusty's throat, following the trail of blood. Lips, very gently, sucked.

Rusty closed his eyes and trembled. Having someone drinking your blood was beyond weird, but it didn't feel bad. It didn't even feel creepy. In fact, the sensuous movements of lips and tongue and the warm weight of Shiro's body pressing full length on top of him was more than a little...stimulating. His breath escaped on a groan.

Shiro swallowed. "That's better." He licked again.

Rusty shifted under Shiro to ease the aching tightness in his jeans. Not that it did any good. Shiro's mouth working against his throat felt way too much like his dream, only...sweeter, almost comforting. Except for the fact that his cock was so damned hard. He bit down on his lip to keep from arching up to rub against the warm belly above him. Good God, why was he so hard?

Shiro swallowed and licked down Rusty's shoulder. He shifted between Rusty's splayed thighs, rubbing what felt like an impressive erection against the seam of Rusty's jeans.

A white-hot bolt of raw pleasure forced a gasp from Rusty's mouth. He grabbed Shiro's ass with both hands to stop his movements, but all it did was press Shiro's erection tighter against Rusty's cock. Shiro's naked erection. He wasn't wearing a damned thing under that robe. A tiny moan of lust escaped.

Shiro leaned up. Scarlet was smeared across his bottom lip. He licked it and smiled. "There you are, the bleeding has stopped."

Rusty hastily released Shiro's ass to grip the cushions under him.

Okay, so Shiro hadn't been lying—about that. "Gee, thanks."

Shiro licked his lips, rising off Rusty's body. "My pleasure."

Rusty took a deep breath in sheer relief that Shiro was finally off his dick. Any more of that and he'd cum in his pants.

Shiro pressed his palms over Rusty's bare chest. "Feeling better?" His fingers found Rusty's nipples. He plucked.

Delight speared straight down into Rusty's cock. It jumped, and he gasped. "Shit!"

Shiro's smile broadened, showing his long teeth. "Ah, I see that you are." He traced his fingers down Rusty's belly to cup his crotch in a hot palm. "And here?" He squeezed.

Heat and lust rocketed up Rusty's spine and detonated in the back of his skull. He arched up hard against Shiro's hand and shouted, "Oh, fuck!"

"That bad?" Shiro licked his lips and tugged at Rusty's belt-buckle, loosening it. "Well, we can't have that."

"Whoa, hey!" Rusty choked and sat up, grabbing for Shiro's wrists "What are you doing now?"

Shiro set his hand over Rusty's heart and shoved, pushing him back down into the cushions. "I would think it's obvious." He plucked Rusty's button open and pulled the zipper downward.

Rusty jerked his knees up and grabbed for his open pants. "Quit that, you perv!"

"No." Shiro slid the hand pressing Rusty into the cushions to the side and trapped a nipple between his thumb and forefinger. At the same time, he moved his other hand into Rusty's open jeans and grasped his cock.

The delicious pinch on his nipple and the warm, snug hand on his dick sent a searing bolt of howling lust straight to Rusty's balls. He threw his head back, gasping.

Shiro eased Rusty's cock free of his jeans, brushing his thumb against the tip of Rusty's cock-head. His thumb came away damp with leaking cum. "Ah, you're weeping for me." He smiled. "How sweet."

"Why?" Rusty trembled among the cushions. "Why are you doing this to me?"

"You need to feed properly." Shiro snug palm stroked Rusty's cock downward from the flared crown to the root, then back up. "Sex is the fastest way to do it."

A groan of sheer animal pleasure exploded from Rusty's throat. His fingers dug into the cushions under him. Shiro's hand felt so damned good.

Shiro released a rumbling sound very like a feline purr. "Oh, that was nice." He leaned over Rusty's body, his lips only a breath away. "Do it again." He gave Rusty's cock a hard, slow pull, then swiped his thumb across the very tip.

Rusty shuddered with the exquisite torment and groaned loudly. He couldn't stop himself.

Shiro pressed his lips over Rusty's open mouth, his tongue surging in and stroking as though seeking to taste the sound.

Rusty stiffened, startled. The invading tongue was gentle, yet thoroughly investigative and he tasted interesting. There was a flavor that hadn't been there before. Rusty stroked his tongue against Shiro's, kissing him back. The flavor of Shiro's kiss became richer and…exciting. He couldn't quite figure out what it was, but it seemed bright, and delicious. He wanted more. He *needed* more.

Shiro's mouth closed tight over Rusty's, his kiss turning demanding, and his hand tightened on Rusty's cock, pumping with strong, slow pulls.

Rolled under by the drugging pleasure of Shiro's exquisite kiss and the skilled hand stroking his cock, Rusty couldn't stop himself from arching up under Shiro, deliberately pushing himself into Shiro's hand, seeking more.

Belly to belly, Shiro groaned and rolled, rubbing the hot length of his cock against Rusty's inner thigh.

Rusty moaned. The hot pressure building in him was overwhelming. He was going to cum…

Shiro curled his fingers around the waistband on the backside of Rusty's jeans. Slowly, he eased them downward.

Cool air washed against Rusty's ass. Startled, Rusty grabbed what few brain cells he had working and jerked his mouth from Shiro's to grab for his pants. "Shiro!"

Shiro rose up on his palms and smiled, his tall ears tipping forward. "Do you really want cum in your jeans?"

Rusty froze, shocked. "I, uh…" He hadn't actually planned to go that far. Hell, he hadn't planned on going *this* far, but…

But he could barely think past the fierce, aching pressure in his balls. There was no way in hell he could stop. Orgasm and the mess that came with it was going to happen, and soon. Heat burned in his cheeks and he swallowed. "No, I don't."

Shiro nodded. "I thought not." He tugged on Rusty's jeans, exposing the full length of his cock, then lower still, past his ass to his thighs.

His face hot with embarrassment Rusty dropped his gaze. His dick was dripping with seepage and his entire body trembled with the urge for release.

Shiro lifted a brow and smiled, then jerked Rusty's jeans all the way down to his ankles and peeled them off, dropping them on the floor.

Rusty flinched. Wearing only his open shirt, vest and socks, he felt so…exposed. He dropped his chin and looked up at Shiro from under his hair. "Happy now?"

Shiro rose to his knees, his robes parting. "Quite." The strong, pale column of an impressive erection arched upward from under the knotted sash, rising from a soft thatch of white curls above his lightly furred ball sack. The flared crown was flushed a rich purple and weeping with eagerness. Shiro was definitely…happy.

Rusty stared. He couldn't help it. He hadn't ever seen anything quite so…lewd. His own cock gave an involuntary jump.

Shiro eased off the longue to stand facing Rusty. He smiled, tilted his head to the side and lifted a brow. "Ready to finish?" He held out his hand.

As if he had a choice? Rusty nodded and took Shiro's hand.

"Good." Shiro tugged Rusty upright onto his feet. "Time to reposition." He tugged his robes to the side, exposing the long muscular line of his bare thigh, and sat back down on the chaise longue, the robes and his huge white tail spilling across the cushions on the far left. Gripping Rusty's hips, Shiro tugged him down onto the cushions to sit between his spread legs.

Sitting between Shiro's naked thighs with the heat of a firm erection pressing against his spine, Rusty swallowed hard. How had he gotten himself into this?

Shiro leaned to Rusty's left. "Now, then…" He set his palm inside Rusty's left thigh and tugged it up over his bare left thigh, spreading Rusty open, then pushed Rusty a bit further over, off his erection. "This way, I can jack you off while you jack me off. Simple, yes?"

Rusty turned slightly to face Shiro and licked his lips. *A mutual jack-off?* He took a deep breath, and looked down at Shiro's pale erection, and then his own rising against his belly. Well, he needed to do something… "Okay."

Shiro smiled. "Good. Touch me."

*Touch him.* Rusty swallowed and twisted to the left. He reached over with his right hand and wrapped his fingers around Shiro's cock. It was smooth as expensive silk and hot against his palm. *Okay, this isn't so bad…* He swept his palm up the long, firm column to the flared crown and brushed his thumb across the damp tip.

Shiro leaned against Rusty's left shoulder, pressing his cheek against Rusty's and sighed. "Mmm, yes. Tighter." He reached over and closed his hand around Rusty's cock, then stroked and squeezed.

The breathtaking torment of Shiro's grip arched Rusty's spine and tore a gasp from his throat. He squeezed Shiro by reflex.

Shiro groaned. "That's more like it." He gripped Rusty's cock and started stroking with fierce strength and ruthless determination.

Rusty pumped Shiro the same way, matching him stroke for stroke. Tension gathered, coiling into a tight, hot knot within him until soft, desperate sounds spilled from his throat. The scent of raw lust filled the air between them.

Shiro's arm tightened around Rusty, drawing him close. "Relax. Don't try to fight it. Just let go."

Panting for breath, Rusty looked up into Shiro's fierce copper gaze and was unable to look away. *Hunger...* He was looking at naked hunger. He shuddered, right on the trembling edge of release.

"That's it. Now..." Shiro smiled, showing teeth, and licked his lips. "Cum for me." He reached around to capture Rusty's nipple and tugged.

Delight speared straight down into Rusty's dick. He gasped, his spine arching, and tumbled into the tight, ferocious clutch of climax. Cum surged, pumping from him in a hot, delicious, mind-numbing spill. He shouted out his release.

Shiro covered Rusty's mouth with his lips, stealing his cries, his tongue surging in to take possession.

Shaking in the wake of his orgasm, Rusty could taste that illusive flavor thick on Shiro's tongue; sweeter than any confection, more potent than the finest whisky. In that moment he knew what it was— it was passion. He was literally tasting Shiro's rising climax. And he wanted it, he *needed* it... A scarlet wave of ravenous, bestial hunger clawed through him.

Rusty locked his free hand in Shiro's hair to hold their mouths together, lapping and sucking, kissing Shiro with utter physical greed. It wasn't enough. More, he needed more... He needed Shiro to cum. His hand tightened on Shiro's cock, stroking mercilessly hard and fast.

Shiro groaned into Rusty's mouth and his eyes closed tight. His cock jumped in Rusty's pumping hand. Cum surged and sprayed, spilling hot thick wetness over Rusty's fist and across his thigh.

Shiro's ecstasy exploded on Rusty's tongue, filling his mouth with a caustic, molten sweetness that seared him. *Too much!* He pushed at Shiro to break the kiss.

Shiro locked his arms around Rusty in blatant refusal, pinning him chest to chest.

Rusty's eyes opened to stare into Shiro's narrowed copper gaze while fire poured down his throat. Shiro was not going to let him go. He shuddered under the burning assault. It speared into his heart, spilling outward into his blood, setting it ablaze. Sweat ran down his body. *Got to stop!* He pushed hard against Shiro's chest, but it was like shoving at a living, breathing brick wall.

A savage growl rumbled in Shiro's chest. Ruthlessly, he pushed Rusty down onto his back among the cushions, pinning him with his body and his burning kiss.

Rusty writhed under him, the flow pouring into him, setting every nerve in his body on fire, scalding him from the inside out, burning him alive. *"No!"* He screamed into Shiro's mouth and raised his knee, jammed it into Shiro's belly, then shoved with all his strength. Claws scored burning lines along his ribs and the sound of ripping fabric was loud.

He broke free and twisted away, rolling off the longue and landing on the floor in a crumpled heap. He stared down at the faded carpet under his cheek, his head spinning as though he'd downed an entire bottle of hard liquor in one sitting.

"Oh, no, you don't!" Shiro lunged off the antique couch, landing on top of him. He wrestled Rusty onto his back and straddled him, pinning him down on the worn carpet. "Drink it, damn you!"

"No!" Rusty kicked out and shoved, but Shiro was too heavy to move. "It's too much!"

"You need it, you idiot!" Shiro grabbed for Rusty's wrists and shoved them down on the floor. "Take it!" He pressed his mouth over Rusty's.

A blazing river of raw flame filled his mouth and poured straight down Rusty's throat. He choked and jerked his head away. "I don't want it!"

"Too bad for you." Shiro bared his teeth and pinned both of Rusty's wrists in one hand. "I will *not* lose you!" He grasped Rusty's jaw, his fingers digging in with punishing strength, forcing Rusty's mouth open. He bared his long teeth, then dropped over him, locking his mouth onto Rusty's.

A torrent of fire spilled into Rusty's mouth and seared down his throat. He arched and bucked under Shiro's weight, but he couldn't break the kiss. Shiro would not let go. The searing essence pouring into him began to churn violently within. Tears streaking down his cheeks, his screams muffled by Shiro's brutal kiss, he submerged under the molten flow of raw ecstasy and was consumed.

# ~ Eight ~

RUSTY JERKED AWAKE AND BLINKED. *WHAT?* HE WAS SLUMPED IN A cushioned chair in the dark. *Where am I?* He pushed upright and squinted into the shadows.

He was sitting in the front row of about three dozen seats set in three curving rows. Right in front of him and only two steps up from the floor was a plain wooden platform maybe twenty strides across with some kind of pitched, shingled roof.

It looked like a theater, an empty theater. He was the only person in there.

*How did I get here?* He grabbed for his chest. He was dressed. His black shirt was buttoned under his vest, his cravat tied, and his jeans were on. He was even wearing the damned flip-flops. *What the hell is this?*

He raised his fingers to his lips. The last thing he remembered was lying under Shiro in his dressing room—and a river of fire pouring down his throat from Shiro's mouth. That had happened after the mutual jack-off session. He pulled his fingers from his face and stared at his hand. Shiro's cock had been so warm… He jammed his hands under his arms. *Never mind that!*

So, how did he get here?

Had he passed out? Had Shiro dressed him? Or, had it all been some kind of a dream?

He sucked on his bottom lip. Shiro's ears, tail and teeth couldn't have been real, so it must have been a dream. A seriously weird dream. But that meant that the mutual jack-off session had been a dream, too, right? He frowned. That hadn't felt like anything like a dream. In fact, he could feel traces of the tension in his muscles from when he came. Hell, his legs were still shaking. He hadn't cum like that in years. His cheeks heated violently. *Quit thinking about that!*

So was it real, or wasn't it?

He swept his hands down his face. He didn't know, he couldn't tell. His fingers brushed the cravat around his shirt collar. The bandage he'd taped to his throat was missing. He jerked the knot free and swept his fingers across the raised flesh that marked his scars. It was dry. He stared at his fingers. Nothing. He wasn't bleeding. But he'd been bleeding all damned day! He squinted at the black cravat in the dark theater, but he couldn't tell if it had any blood on it.

Oh wait… Shiro had taken the bandage off. He winced. To drink his blood. All the really weird shit had happened right after that; the tail and ears, the sex, the burning kiss… So, was *that* part real, and the rest a dream? Had he hallucinated from blood-loss?

But he wasn't bleeding anymore. He couldn't even feel a scab to show that he'd been bleeding in the first place. *What in hell is going on?*

A hard knock from a wood block echoed in the empty theater, then another, then another. A strong masculine voice ululated, filling the darkness with his resonating voice.

*Huh?* Rusty jerked upright in his seat. *What is this?*

A stringed instrument sounding kind of like a weird cross between a violin and a sitar started playing something distinctly cheerful. Deep, sad notes from a softly blown flute whispered almost invisibly under the merry music of the strings.

Rusty's brows lifted. He was pretty sure the stringed instrument was an oriental samisen.

Thumping footsteps came from the far left. Someone walked toward the stage, carrying what looked like a square paper lantern bouncing at the end of a slender pole. The light spilled across drab brown knee-length robes held closed with an intricately knotted hunk of white rope. An unruly mop of scarlet hair bounced atop his head and around his shoulders.

Rusty blinked. Was this a *Noh* play? He hadn't actually seen one before, but he'd read up on Japanese theater while researching the costumes he'd made. The young man was dressed in the costume of the standard character known as Youth, though he wasn't sure Youth was supposed to have *red* hair.

Youth took center stage and posed, his lantern raised to the level of his cheek, and his other hand fisted on his hip, the picture of insolent boredom.

The lights came up, filling the roofed stage with near daylight brightness. The back wall of the stage was painted with an extravagantly twisted cedar tree and ornate clouds. Against the wall, as though shaded by the cedar tree, sat the orchestra. Five musicians dressed in black robes, all kneeling on thick black pillows and holding instruments that dated back to the medieval era.

*Huh...* Rusty sat back in his chair. It really was a *Noh* play, or something like it. *Noh* characters normally wore wooden masks. Well, this was the Oriental Playhouse and Shiro had mentioned something about historical plays. He swallowed. *Adult* historical plays.

The wood block knocked three times, then three more times just a bit faster, then three more times even faster. The wood-block musician, a rather robust and completely bald man, called out in his deep voice. "Yoooooiiii!" His call ended on an impressively high pitch.

A slender older gentleman with a deeply receding hairline, wearing a particularly ugly set of black-framed glasses, raised a large bamboo flute to his lips. The flute moaned.

Rhythmic thumping from the far left announced another actor heading for the stage down the long wooden walkway. The figure bounced, literally prancing up on his toes, his hands curled before him like paws. A snow-white grinning Fox mask was tied to his face.

Rusty leaned back. *So, that's why Youth wasn't wearing a mask.* He'd read somewhere that only time the human characters in this kind of a play *didn't* wear masks was when a Fox was in the play, too.

Apparently having a fox in the play could cause the other masks to become haunted—because all foxes, even in plays, were considered spirits.

*Kitsune...*

A hard shiver raced up his spine.

An older woman, her black hair coiled decoratively on the top of her head, raised a tall stringed instrument. Beside her, a very slender middle-aged woman with her dark hair also coiled on her head raised her smaller stringed instrument. The cheerful tune bounced into play, accompanying the flute.

Fox skidded to a stop at the edge of the stage, his hands flying up in clear surprise. The music skidded to a stop with him. Long silver hair flowed down his back, blending nearly perfectly with his floor-length iridescent white robes and the enormous white foxtail that rose from the split in Fox's fluttering robes.

Youth, two steps forward and looking the other way, did not see him.

Rusty gripped the arms of his chair. He knew that white robe. He knew that tail. It was Shiro, and his white mask *was* identical to the black fox he'd carved. *Oh, fuck...*

*"I'm a Kitsune, a fox spirit. You'd think the ears and tail would give that away."*

His hands flying to his cheeks, Fox faced the audience, his huge tail whisking from side to side.

Tiny bells jingled in the hand of a young lady, her dark hair coiled on the top of her head and tied with a decorative ribbon.

Fox turned back to Youth, set one hand on his hip and leaned back on his heels. Tilting his head from one side to the other, he stroked the chin of his grinning muzzle. Abruptly he raised a finger, then pressed his open palm to the end of his muzzle. He turned to the audience and hunched, his shoulders bouncing in the exaggerated motions of someone laughing.

The woodblock knocked once.

Youth turned toward Fox and pointed, clearly astounded.

Fox threw up his hands and tripped back a step, apparently just as astounded.

Youth set his lantern on the floor, then opened his arms wide, lifted them, and crooked his fingers for a grab.

The strings made a cheerful, but clearly hesitant start.

Fox leaned back, extending his arms palm out.

The woodblock knocked twice.

Lifting his foot very high, Youth stepped toward Fox.

Fox lifted his foot very high and stepped back from Youth.

The strings made another start, and the bells jingled.

Youth took another huge step toward Fox.

Fox took another huge step to the side, toward the back of the stage.

The woodblock knocked three times.

Youth lunged after Fox.

Fox threw up his hands and bolted.

The strings and flute bounced into merry play.

Arms outstretched, Youth chased the arm-waving and far faster Fox all the way around the stage in a huge circle. Fox ran so fast that on the third circle, Fox came up behind Youth and grabbed him around the waist, pressing his cheek against Youth's spine.

The music crashed to a disorganized and startled halt.

They both froze in the middle of the stage, Youth's outstretched arms still posed for a grab and Fox's arms around his middle. Youth turned slowly to look at the audience, his eyes wide and a deep frown on his face.

Fox snuggled against Youth's lower back, his upraised tail waving gently.

The robust gentleman picked up a drum and thumped a slow tempo that gained in speed, then stopped.

Youth stiffened, then set his hands on his hips and turned around in Fox's embrace. With his fist, Youth knocked on top of Fox's head, the woodblock sounding with each hit.

Hunched over, Fox flinched, looked up at Youth and jerked his hands behind him.

Youth set his hands on Fox's shoulders and firmly pushed him back.

Fox tripped back a step, one hand over the end of his muzzle, the other curled in the manner of a paw.

Youth shook his finger at Fox, then turned to the audience. He raised his chin, rolled his shoulders and wiped his hands down each sleeve. Setting his hands on his hips and striking a very manly pose, Youth looked over at Fox, then looked away in an obvious snub.

The flute wailed out a dignified air while the strings plinked out the merry melody behind it.

Fox jerked completely upright, his hands fisting at his sides, and his tail pointed straight up. He stomped his foot, clearly pissed.

The woodblock knocked once.

Youth tipped to the side, off-balance, his arms flailing. He gained his footing and faced Fox, his hands flying to his cheeks in alarm.

Fox raised his arms, opening them wide, and crooked his fingers for a grab.

The flute moaned, and tiny bells jingled.

Youth leaned back, extending his arms palm out. He shook his head.

Lifting his foot very high, Fox nodded quite firmly, then stepped toward Youth.

The woodblock knocked twice.

Youth lifted his foot very high and stepped back from Fox.

The strings made a hesitant start, and the bells jingled.

The woodblock knocked three times, then three more times just a bit faster, then three more times even faster. The robust member of the orchestra called out in his deep voice and his drum throbbed in a marching beat.

Fox and Youth froze in position.

Loud, slow thumping from the far left announced that yet another actor was slow-marching down the long walkway toward the stage, his steps in time with the drum.

Youth and Fox turned to stare toward stage left, then leaned with their hands over their eyes to see who was coming.

The newcomer wore a small black hat perched on his head, with his long black hair drawn back into a tail that bounced against his back. His blatantly patched red and yellow robes were tucked into flowing trousers of bright green. Over his shoulder, he carried the short bow of a forest hunter.

Fox and Youth leaned back. They turned slowly toward each other and stared at each other, their mouths covered by their palms.

The deep voice sang out.

Fox and Youth threw up their hands in alarm.

The flute and strings bounced into a mad, jouncing tune.

Youth and Fox bolted around in a tight, panicked circle until they slammed into each other, chest to chest, and wrapped their arms around each other in obvious fright, facing the audience, with Fox's arms below Youth's.

The jouncing tune crashed to a halt.

The flute moaned, and tiny bells jingled.

Fox snuggled, rubbing his cheek against Youth's chest.

Youth looked down at Fox and waved his hands in complete shock. He pushed at the Fox.

Fox moved back to the extent of his arms' reach, then slammed back into Youth, embracing him with his arms repositioned to pin Youth's arms to his sides.

Youth shook his head and rolled his eyes, then stomped his foot in clear annoyance.

The flute moaned, and tiny bells jingled.

Fox looked straight at the Youth, tipped up his mask with his off hand and planted his lips on Youth's lips, kissing him.

The flute played a hauntingly sweet melody.

His arms supposedly trapped by Fox, Youth's hands splayed open. His foot came up in back and shook, clearly affected by the kiss.

The melody ended.

Fox dropped his mask back into place, and snuggled against

Youth's shoulder, apparently pleased with himself.

Youth turned to stare at the audience wearing a deep frown, his eyes wide with horror. He threw his head back and wriggled frantically in Fox's embrace, his red hair flying every which way. The strings wailed with his struggles. He pulled one arm free, and then the other. Once both arms were free, he made a fist and konked Fox on top of the head. The woodblock knocked at the same time.

Fox flinched under the blow, but didn't let go. Instead, he slid down to Youth's waist.

The flute moaned, and tiny bells jingled.

Fox turned and pressed the point of his muzzle against Youth's rope belt, then knocked against it with his nose three times, clearly imitating a blowjob.

Youth threw up his hands in overwhelming alarm and struggled in Fox's arms.

The orchestra bounced into a merry if slightly awkward tune.

Fox faced the audience, completely unaffected.

Youth writhed, kicked and twisted until he had turned completely around. He stopped cold, bent over with Fox's arms locked around his hips, leaning over his back.

The merry tune jerked to a halt.

The flute moaned, and tiny bells jingled.

Still staring at the audience, Fox twitched his robes to either side of Youth's hips, then slow-humped Youth's backside three times. The woodblock knocked in perfect tempo.

Youth turned to the audience and slapped both hands over his mouth.

The drums crashed into a sudden and ferocious tempo, and the bald man yowled. The Hunter had arrived on the stage.

Fox and Youth jerked upright and apart, with Fox turning away and making a fuss of straightening his robes before turning back.

The Hunter posed on the edge of the stage, drew back his bowstring and pointing a long black arrow at Fox.

The flute moaned, and tiny bells jingled.

Fox pointed at his chest.

Hunter nodded firmly.

Fox turned to Youth, bowed and stepped back to the center of the stage to face the Hunter's arrow.

Youth looked from Fox to Hunter, then back at Fox.

The drum pounded out a furious rhythm.

Fox tugged on his lapels and lifted his chin toward Hunter.

Youth grabbed his scarlet hair and jumped up and down while tugging on it.

The strings began to play the sweet melody that the flute had carried before.

Youth made a dramatic leap, landing facing Fox with his arms outstretched, putting himself before Hunter's arrow.

Seated right before the stage, Rusty's heart hammered achingly hard in his chest. The shadows of a nightmare screamed at the edges of his mind.

The drums crashed to a halt.

Hunter released his bowstring.

Youth jerked forward, falling into Fox's arms, the black arrow protruding from his back.

Pain stabbed through Rusty's heart as though something was lodged there, trying to stop it from beating. He gasped and clutched at his chest.

Staring at Fox, Youth dropped to his knees, red silk spilling from the front of his robes.

The strings and the flute played the haunting melody with slow poignant sadness.

Hunter threw up his arms in horror, and ran back down the walkway.

# ~ *Nine* ~

*T*HE SWEET, SLOW MELODY FILLED THE SHADOWED THEATER.

In the center of the antique stage, the white-robed Fox dropped to his knees, pulling the arrow-shot Youth across his lap. Scarlet silk unraveled from Youth's robes to become a deep red blanket across Youth's chest.

Fox took Youth's chin and turned Youth's face to him.

Youth reached up to clutch Fox's white robes.

Rusty's chest throbbed as though something was trying to rip it apart from the inside. He closed his eyes and gasped for breath.

"Do you want to live?" It sounded like a little boy.

"Of course I want to live, idiot." This voice came from a somewhat older boy. He chuckled very softly. "But it doesn't look like that's going to happen.

*It hurts!* Rusty hunched over, tears spilling down his cheeks. *God, it hurts!*

"I can save you, but it will cost you."

The boy gasped for breath and coughed. "What do you want, my soul?"

"And your heart. I want your heart and soul. Will you give them to me?"

"Sure." The older boy coughed. "It's not like I'm gonna be using them." His voice was soft, barely there.

"Kiss me."

Rusty's eyes opened.

Onstage, Fox had pushed up his mask to kiss Youth full on the mouth. In his free hand was another mask, a black fox—Rusty's

60

mask. Shiro turned to look straight at Rusty, sitting in the audience. His copper eyes were hard and his mouth grim. He set the black fox over the face of Youth. "It is done. You are mine."

Rusty's heart blazed with sudden heat, pumping raw flame into his veins and setting his body on fire. His spine arched, jerking him upright in the chair.

In the autumn of his senior year, he'd taken a walk in the woods. The trees had been red and gold with the turn of the season, and the air had carried the scent of wood smoke.

A white fox crossed his path.

*How incredibly cool!* He'd never seen a solid white fox before. He turned off the path to follow it. Running hunched over among the last of the summer's growth, he couldn't see more than a couple of feet ahead of him, but he could see the fox. Moving no faster than a trot through the underbrush, the fox's bright tail was easy to trail among all the green and brown.

Scuttling through a screen of bushes, the ground dropped out from under his feet and he tumbled down a hill to landing in a heap at the bottom of small depression.

A boy in pale blue faded jeans and a white T-shirt skidded down the hill to kneel at his side. His long hair was snowy white. "Are you okay?"

His hands were scraped, and he had bruised knees, but that was nothing. He wiped his palms together and smiled sourly at the kid. "Nah, I'm fine." He frowned at the white-haired kid. "Do you live around here? I don't remember you."

The kid grinned. "Nope, I'm just visiting."

He pushed to his feet and brushed the dirt from his knees. "You're not lost or anything, are you?"

The kid blinked. "Who, me?" He snorted. "I don't get lost."

"Is that so?" He held out his hand. "Well, I'm Russ, short for

Russell."

The kid smiled and took his hand. "Nice to meet you, Russ."

"Nice to meet you, too." Russ grinned and gave the kid's hand a shake. *Cute kid.* "Hang on to me and I'll get us out of here."

The kid's fingers closed around Russ's hand with surprising strength. "Sure."

Russ started up the hill, tugging the kid up the hill behind him. "You going to school around here?"

The kid laughed. "No, I'm just visiting."

Russ grinned down at him. "Oh, yeah, that's right." He looked behind them to the far side of the depression. Something long and black was sticking out of the bushes hanging over the edge. It was the barrel of a rifle, and it was pointed straight at the kid. "No!" Russ twisted and dove on top of him. "Get down!"

Something exploded, and ripped through his back. And then he was falling. And falling...

Someone was shouting in his ear. "Russ? Russell?"

*Huh?* Russ opened his eyes to find the kid leaning over him with tears in his eyes. Russ frowned. "What happened?"

The kid turned away, rubbing the back of his fist across his cheek. "I'm... I'm sorry."

"Hey, don't..." Russ raised his hand to wipe away the kid's tears. Pain ripped through his entire chest. He tried to shout, but he didn't have enough air to do more than groan. "It...hurts." He had to close his eyes, just for a second...or two.

"You got shot. The guy that shot you ran away."

Oh, so that where all the pain was coming from, a bullet. Russ opened his eyes and frowned. "The guy ran...away?"

The kid's eyes were closed tight. "He said it was an accident. He wasn't aiming for you."

"An...accident." Russ smiled in spite of the pain. "That makes me feel so much...better." He had to stop to breathe, but breathing hurt. It hurt a lot. It felt like he was being stabbed with every breath. "Ah..."

The kid looked him dead in the eye, tears trickling down his cheeks. "You're dying."

Russ sucked in a tiny breath and stilled. *Dying? He couldn't mean like, seriously dying?* But he was so warm… He looked down at his shirt. It was really, really red and wet. It was blood. His blood, and a lot of it. It was coming out of this hole in his shirt. "Oh…" He coughed and pain stabbed through him. He moaned. *Fuck, that hurt!* Well, maybe the kid had a point. He took a small breath. "Dying, okay, great." He looked at the kid's face. He really didn't want to watch all that blood coming out of him. The kid was much nicer to look at.

The kid leaned close. "Do you want to live?"

"Huh?" He winced. Damn it, talking hurt, and it was so hard to breathe. He took a couple of small shallow breaths. "Of course I want to live, idiot." He chuckled very softly, and it hurt. A lot. He gasped, and that hurt, too. "But it doesn't look like that's going to happen." His eyes watered and tears slipped down his cheeks.

The kid sucked on his bottom lip. "I can save you, but it will cost you."

Russ sucked in a couple of shallow breaths, but there was something in his lungs. He coughed. Blood spattered from his mouth. "Ow." He took in a smaller breath. "What do you want, my soul?" The words came out in a whisper. He just didn't have enough air to spare.

The kid set his warm palm on Russ's brow. "And your heart. I want your heart and soul. Will you give them to me?"

"Sure." Russ tried to smile, but it was kinda hard to do with this dying thing hanging over his head. Fuck, he hadn't even graduated from high school or had sex yet. He took a tiny breath and let his tears fall. "It's not like I'm gonna be using them."

The kid leaned over Russ. "Kiss me."

Russ looked up at him and cracked a smile, even though it hurt. "You're kidding, right?"

The kid wiped at his damp cheek. "No."

"You're not…" Russ tried to pull in a full breath but it hurt too much. "You're not supposed to…" He wheezed for air. "Kiss somebody you don't love." His voice came out a whisper.

The kid smiled. "Then I'll love you."

Russ tried to laugh in spite of the pain in his chest and the tears dripping from his chin. "Okay." He closed his eyes and felt the press of warm, soft lips against his.

The pain eased until it was nothing more than a fading echo.

# ~ *Ten* ~

**R**USTY SIGHED IN RELIEF AND OPENED HIS EYES. HE WAS IN HIS SEAT IN THE theater, though the stage was silent and dark but for a single paper lantern sitting on the very edge. He wiped at the tears streaking down his cheeks. He'd been rifle shot. How had he forgotten? Never mind that, how had he survived?

Shiro leaned over him in the silk robes, his white hair falling over them both. He still had ears and a tail. "Now do you remember me, Russ?"

Rusty took in a careful breath. His chest still ached, though it was fading. "You were that kid in the woods?" He wiped at his cheeks. Why couldn't he stop crying?

Shiro smiled. "And the fox." He looked away and his smile evaporated. "If you hadn't followed me, you wouldn't have gotten hurt."

Rusty snorted. "I wasn't about to let a kid get shot."

Shiro's brows lifted and one ear cocked to the side. "So you took the bullet yourself?"

Rusty shrugged. "Um...yeah."

Shiro's mouth curved up into a dreamy smile. "So impulsive, so brave..."

Rusty looked away and wiped at his chin. He wasn't brave. Truthfully, he hadn't thought the guy would shoot.

Shiro pressed a warm palm to Rusty's cheek and wiped at the traces of tears. "You took a bullet meant for me. I couldn't let you die."

Rusty stilled. His heart thumped in his chest and heat flooded his cheeks. Shiro's gentle touch felt good, it felt…comforting. He winced away from Shiro's hand. He was thinking weird thoughts again. He rubbed at his chest and frowned. "There's no mark, no scar from the gunshot wound."

"Of course not." Shiro smiled. "I remade you." His fingers slid down to Rusty's throat, delivering shivers. "The only mark you will ever bear—is mine."

That bite. He still didn't remember getting it, just the kiss… Rusty winced. "Please tell me I didn't have sex with a minor?"

Shiro chuckled. "No, we didn't do that. I bit you."

Rusty smiled sourly. "You mean, like a werewolf? You bit me, and now I'm like you?"

"Not exactly." Shiro sighed and looked down. "I bit you to get into your body so I could pull out your soul and put in…something else."

Something *else?* A black hole opened around Rusty's heart. "What are you saying?"

"Same thing I've been telling you all along." Shiro smiled sadly. "You're not human, that's why you can't live as one. You don't belong among them."

Rusty jerked back. "Don't belong?" That didn't make any sense at all. "Why the hell not?"

Shiro sighed. "The human world is made up of very delicate checks and balances. What we are, disturbs that balance."

Rusty frowned in confusion. "Disturbs it, in what way?"

Shiro shrugged. "Oh, the usual. From simple messing with the weather and power outages to major accidents and death."

*Oh…* Rusty swallowed. "Usual, huh?"

"The human world is incredibly delicate." Shiro gave him a crooked smile. "We give off a lot of energy and it tends to make things happen around us. Kind of like power surges. We short-out pockets of the system."

Rusty pushed up in the chair. "So where am I supposed to go? I have a life here…"

Shiro smiled. "You'll be with me. I'll take good care of you."

Rusty shook his head. "I can take care of myself."

Shiro's gaze narrowed and he caught Rusty's wrist. "The way you have been, by starving?" His hand tightened. "I made you, I'm responsible for you and for the damage your presence causes."

Rusty jerked his arm away. "What are you, my mother?"

Shiro's eyes narrowed and his ears flattened back to his skull. "What I am is your sire, and you are my consort. You belong with me."

"Your consort?" As in a *kept lover*? Rusty bared his teeth. "Are you telling me that my purpose in life is to take your dick up my ass?"

Shiro bared his long teeth as well. "If you want to see it that way, then, yeah."

Rusty jerked upright. "Fuck that shit!" He came out of the chair and shoved past Shiro, stomping over to the lantern at the edge of the stage. "Go find some other ass for your dick!"

In a whisper of white silk, Shiro came up behind Rusty and grabbed him by the upper arm, his long nails digging in. He jerked Rusty around to face him. "I already have one, and I'm keeping it."

"Don't you get it?" Rusty glared at him. "I don't want *any* dick up my ass!"

"What you don't get…" Shiro tugged Rusty against his chest and caught the hair at the back of his head. "Is that you need me." He took Rusty's mouth in a harsh kiss.

The taste of Shiro, as fierce and potent as whisky, speared straight down, stirring hot shivers down his spine. Excitement bloomed, filling his cock and weakening his knees. Rusty moaned and grabbed for Shiro's shoulders, clutching his robes to keep from falling. The kiss burned from his tongue all the way down to his balls, erasing every thought in his head but the urge to lay down and…and fuck.

Shiro broke the kiss and pulled him into a tight embrace. "Rusty, damn it… It's not supposed to be like this. Stop fighting me."

Rusty closed his eyes, dropping his head on Shiro's shoulder. *Shit, shit, shit…* He took shallow breaths, trying to get a grip on his hammering heart and the violent throbbing in his dick. "Damn you..." His fingers tightened in Shiro's robes. "Why are you doing this to me?"

Shiro's arms tightened around him. "I love you, you stupid fuck. Why do you think I couldn't let you die? Why do you think I kept looking for you?"

*Love? Jeez...* Rusty groaned, his entire body trembling. "You can't love me. You don't even know me." God, his dick ached. It took everything in him to resist the urge to rub his aching cock against Shiro's hip for even the tiniest bit of relief.

Shiro snorted. "Sure I can. I've loved you since the day you took that bullet for me, and you love me, too."

"I've never loved anybody. I don't think I'm capable of it." Rusty turned his head to Shiro's neck, the long silver hair sliding sensuously through his fingers. God, he smelled good.

Shiro leaned back to stare into Rusty's eyes. "You love me. You just need to realize it." He pressed a kiss to Rusty's mouth, his lips gentle this time, his tongue coaxing.

Rusty's will to resist drowned under a hot wash of naked lust. He closed his arms around Shiro. Moaning in pure desperation, he reached up and fisted one hand in all that rich silver hair and slid the other down to cup Shiro's ass. He pressed his hips full against him, cock to cock, and rubbed.

Shiro slid his hands down to cup Rusty's ass, then broke the kiss. "That's better. Much better." He stroked the wet velvet of his tongue along the length of Rusty's throat. "Do you want to cum?"

Rusty trembled, his eyes closing and his head falling back, letting Shiro's mouth make magic on his skin. "Yes."

Sharp teeth raked against Rusty's throat. "Say please."

The minor pain made Rusty's belly clench and his dick jump with eagerness. He gasped. "Please!"

"Good." Shiro pressed a soft kiss over the small hurt. He reached back, pulled Rusty's hand off his ass and brought it to the front and beneath his robes. He curled Rusty's fingers around the base of his cock.

Rusty stroked Shiro's smooth, rigid length without being asked.

Shiro groaned against his throat. "Yes, very nice." He tightened his arms around Rusty and his lips brushed against Rusty's ear. "Ask me to fuck you."

The fog of lust retreated just enough for Rusty to realize what Shiro had just said. He jerked his head back and stared. "Say…what?"

Shiro smiled but his eyes narrowed to blazing copper slits. "Ask me to fuck you." He closed his hand around Rusty's hand around his cock. "Tell me you want this dick in your ass."

Rusty dropped his head scowling. *Bastard!* He was actually desperate enough to let Shiro take it, but he couldn't—he wouldn't—volunteer for it. He pulled his hand off Shiro's dick, and stepped back, shaking his head. "You didn't need it before."

"That was before." Shiro folded his arms and smiled viciously, showing the full length of his impressive fangs. "This is now." His tall ears fell back against his skull. "If you want to cum, there's only one way it's going to happen, and you're going to have to ask for it."

"Bullshit." Rusty crossed his arms and glared at Shiro. "I've got a hand; I'll take care of it myself."

"I'm afraid handling it yourself isn't an option." Shiro's chin dropped, though his smile remained. "Not with my cock-ring on you."

"What?" Rusty frowned. "A cock-ring?" He grabbed his crotch, feeling for a band of some kind around the base of his dick. "I don't feel anything…" Not through his jeans, anyway.

Shiro shrugged. "You're not going to. It's a spell designed specifically to keep you from reaching orgasm."

"A spell—on my dick?" Rusty bit back a chuckle. "You really expect me to believe in magic?"

Shiro tilted his head slightly and his tail switched from side to side. "Oh, I'd say it's about as believable as my ears and tail."

Rusty swallowed. Shiro's ears and tail were pretty damned

believable. "How long is this spell of yours supposed to last?"

"It'll last as long as it takes." Shiro turned away and looked over his shoulder. "I waited years to get you back, I can wait a few more days to get you in bed."

"Days?" The hair on Rusty's neck rose. *Days* of not being able to cum?

"*If* it takes that long." Shiro's smile turned decided vicious. "You're not cumming until I let you, and I'm not letting you until you offer me your ass."

"Fuck!" He'd had enough of this. Rusty turned, stepping away and scowled into the deep shadows. The tiny paper lantern was the only source of light. The rest of the theater was so damned dark he had no clue where the exit was. "Why?" He turned back and faced Shiro. "Why are you fucking with my head like this?"

"The only one fucking with your head—is you." Shiro stepped over to the stage and lifted the paper lantern. "It's time you stopped running away from what you really are, and what you really want." He turned to face Rusty and the light shifted around him, becoming an indistinct glare.

*Huh?* Rusty squinted, but Shiro's figure continued to go hazy. Was something wrong with his eyes? He rubbed them.

Shiro came back into focus, but his robes, ears and tail were gone. He was merely the tall, cool-looking blond guy from before with his hair, drawn into a snug tail, falling over the shoulder of his pale gray leather coat. He even wore the same gray sweater and dark dress pants. Shiro lifted the small paper lantern to the level of his cheek. "I've chased you long enough. This time, you will come to me." He turned, and blew out the light.

Darkness smothered everything and the ground tipped under Rusty's feet. He fell.

And fell...

# ~ Eleven ~

*"...you will come to me."*

RUSTY JERKED AWAKE, AND THE BACK OF HIS HEAD THUNKED ON A HARD, somewhat hollow surface. "Ow, shit..." He was flat on his back in darkness with some kind of weighted blanket tossed over him. He sat up slowly, rubbing the back of his skull. Whatever he was on was smooth, like a...table?

He shoved at the heavy blanket and recognized the scratchy wool. It was his coat. A quick exploration proved that he still had his clothes on. That was a relief. But his shoes were missing. He waggled his stocking toes. He wasn't even wearing those silly flip-flops.

So, where was he? He glanced around. Thin gray light came through curtains covering a row of windows. The shadows looked suspiciously familiar, and he could hear the groaning wheeze of an old furnace. He was in his workshop, sitting on top of the cutting table.

Rusty scruffed his fingers through his hair and frowned. Had the whole thing been some kind of dream or hallucination? The play? The sex? The ears and tail? Had Shiro slipped him something in that beer at the restaurant? He absently scratched the side of his neck and his fingers stilled on the ridges of his scars. The cravat was still undone and the bandage was still missing. He swallowed. *Uh...*

Never mind that, how the hell had he gotten here? Rusty twisted around to sit on the table's edge. Had Shiro carried him all the way into the basement? If he had, how had he gotten through the locked doors?

Was he sure he wanted to know?

Rusty shook his head firmly. However it had happened, he was back where he belonged, and it was over. *Thank God.*

He slid off the table and landed on something that rolled under his feet. He tipped off-balance and grabbed for the edge of the table. Carefully, he reached down to feel for what he'd stepped on. His shoes. *Oh.*

He took a careful walk across the crammed room toward the windows. What the hell time was it? He turned on the standing lamp in front of the Singer machine and winced in the sudden glare. The clock by the sewing machine said that it was just after two in the morning. He frowned. Why was it so light outside? He shoved open a curtain.

Snow, everywhere. Thick clumps fell from the pale gray sky with at least a foot and a half already on the ground. The branches on the trees were defined by at least an inch.

Rusty groaned. The season's first blizzard. *Great.* He sighed. There was no way in hell he could drive home in this. He smiled sourly. "Anybody got a dog-sled I can borrow?" He pulled the curtain all the way open. He was stuck at the shop, but at least the view was nice. He scratched the back of his head. Odd, he didn't remember any mention of snow in the weather reports.

He turned to look back at the table. Yep, those were his shoes kicked over at the foot of the table, and his knapsack was right next to them. He was glad he'd stepped on his shoes. One step to the right and he would have landed on the bag and snapped the fragile wooden fox mask inside.

Stretching, Rusty made his way upstairs. The shop was an old Victorian house, complete with a full bathroom and a working kitchen. He wouldn't freeze and he wouldn't starve. A nice hot shower, a change of clothes, and a couple of hours of sleep on the futon by the furnace would do him a world of good.

As soon as he got rid of his erection.

"Fuck!" Standing in the shower in the shop's old tile bathroom, Rusty stared at his stubborn erection while the shower's spray got steadily colder. He'd run the boiler out of hot water. He been jacking at his dick for a good twenty minutes, at least, but he wasn't any closer to dumping his load. He was right the fuck there, but nothing he did or imagined could finish him.

Scowling, he shut off the water, looked up at the ceiling and started shouting. "Shiro, you son of a fucking bitch…!"

Not that it helped.

Officially pissed off to the max, Rusty dragged on a black company sweatshirt, fresh out of the plastic, a pair of black sweat pants he'd left there to sleep in, and some fresh socks. He padded out of the bathroom and into the kitchen to toss his jeans in the washing machine, then dug in the cabinets for sandwich makings and some soup to heat.

Sitting at the scarred up circular kitchen table, a roast-beef sandwich in one hand and the soupspoon in the other, Rusty contemplated his situation. He had an erection he couldn't get rid of; and the foul temper that went with it. There was no way in hell he could sleep like this.

He took a bite from his sandwich and dipped his spoon into the pot of beef and noodle soup. He hadn't bothered with a bowl; he was afraid he'd break it. He'd already bent two spoons just by holding them too hard. He needed to do something to work off his temper before he broke something out of sheer frustration. But what?

He looked out the window at the falling snow, and smiled.

An hour later, Rusty walked out the shop's back door and tramped down the steps snug in his black wool coat, with a black cowboy hat perched on his head and a red and green Santa's Helper muffler around his neck. His freshly washed and dried jeans were tucked into a pair of big rubber Santa Claus boots and the furry Barney the Bear hands made nice warm gloves. Determined, he crunched through the thick snow covering the back parking lot to the side of the building. He unlocked the door to the storage closet and pulled out the snow shovel.

Yeah, it was two in the morning and anything he accomplished would be completely obliterated by nine a.m., but that wasn't the point. The point was to work off some of his frustration. Shoveling snow in the middle of a blizzard should accomplish that nicely, not to mention that the cold ought to do something about his erection, too.

Rusty gritted his teeth and started shoveling the front walk. "Fuck magic!"

Three hours later, the snow was still coming down non-stop and all the shoveling had of course, filled right back in with only a slight indentation to show that someone had at least tried. The snowman he'd stopped to build was gaining in inches, too.

But he was finally tired enough to sleep and best of all, the erection was gone due to the overwhelming cold.

His teeth chattering, Rusty grinned up at the falling snow and shouted. "Magic, my ass!" He jabbed his middle finger at the sky for good measure. He tramped back into the shop and pulled off of his cowboy hat, coat, muffler, bear paws and boots with a sense of accomplishment. At last he could get some sleep!

Chilled to the bone, Rusty tossed his snow-melt-soaked jeans back into the wash along with the sweatshirt, then took another hot shower to warm up. He dragged on a clean sweatshirt, put his sweatpants back on, then thumped down the steps to the basement. Completely exhausted, he stumbled toward the furnace and dropped face-first onto the futon against the back wall. Yawning, he dragged the scratchy green woolen army blanket over him and snuggled into his pillow. He was asleep in seconds.

Warmth, comfort, softness…stroking down his back. It felt…nice. Rusty sighed. It felt like…a hand? He frowned. *A dream?*

"Yes, a dream." There was a soft familiar masculine chuckle. "Of sorts."

*Shiro!* Rusty clenched his eyes closed, one hand gripping the scratchy blanket, the other clutching his pillow. *Go away! I don't want to dream about you.*

Breath brushed against Rusty's ear. "Oh, now, that's a shame, because I definitely wish to dream about you." A wet tongue swept across the back of Rusty's neck.

Rusty shivered. *Damn it!* He dragged the scratchy wool up over his head. *I'm trying to get some sleep here!*

"But, Rusty, you *are* asleep."

*Huh?* The blanket evaporated from Rusty's grasp—and his clothes with it. He was naked and lying facedown on what felt like silk sheets. "What the...?" He twisted sharply, flipping over onto his back.

Propped up on his hands and framing Rusty's shoulders, Shiro smiled down at Rusty from only a kiss away. He was completely naked, kneeling to either side of Rusty's hips. His tall fox ears lifted, parting his long silky hair. The frost-white strands fell loose past his bare shoulders and muscular arms, framing a rather nice if milk-pale chest with erect and blushing nipples. The white, fluffy tail was back too, waving gently from side to side. "Hello, love."

Rusty's heart thumped hard. The two of them were in some kind of round, canopied bed draped in silvery gray silk and mounded with pillows. The bed was a little hard to focus on, and everything beyond the bed was completely hazy. The only thing clear and distinct was Shiro. "Whoa... Some dream."

Shiro grinned, showing the tips of his long teeth. "You say the sweetest things."

Rusty folded his arms over his bare chest. "Great, I'm dreaming. Now what?"

Shiro lowered his head slowly, his sumptuous hair sweeping across Rusty's chest. "Take a wild guess." Shiro's lips brushed against Rusty's in clear invitation.

Rusty lifted his chin and opened his mouth to taste the warm wet velvet of Shiro's tongue. The leisurely strokes wiped all thought from his brain. *God, he's good at this...* He moaned and reached up to sink his fingers into all that silky hair.

Shiro moaned in obvious appreciation and pulled back to lap along Rusty's bottom lip. "What? No resistance?"

Rusty's cheeks heated ferociously. "It's just a dream, right?"

"Ah..." Shiro mouth tilted up into a slight smile. "Then you do want me, even if it's only in your dreams?" He leaned down to nibble on Rusty's throat.

Rusty shivered and groaned, raising his chin to let Shiro's mouth make magic against his throat. "Um, yeah." It was dealing with the waking reality of lusting after a guy that he had problems with.

"Mmm..." Shiro eased down Rusty's body to lap at his nipples, stirring bright, hot sparks of delight. "That's nice to know."

Rusty trembled under Shiro's skillful tongue and nipping teeth. *No, that's not right.* He didn't want *a* guy, he wanted *this* guy. He slid his arms around Shiro's broad shoulders, exploring the firm muscle under his fingers. He wanted this strange, beautiful and exciting guy. *Shiro...* No one else, female or male, made his blood race, his heart pound or stirred his body—not to mention his temper—the way Shiro did. When he was with Shiro, he felt awake, he felt...*alive.*

But, what the hell was he supposed to do about it? Rusty groaned and shook his head. Everything was all messed up in his mind.

Shiro slid his hand under Rusty's right knee, pushing it up, spreading him open. "Relax, Rusty, love is not as complicated as you seem to think."

Rusty blinked. *Huh?* Was he thinking out loud or something?

"What if you are?" Shiro chuckled. "This is just a dream, remember?" He eased between Rusty's spread thighs, lying on top of him, belly against belly, his cock a hot, rigid length alongside Rusty's. "Let go and just enjoy your dream."

Heat flushed down Rusty's body in a mind-numbing, erotic wave, his brain refusing to concentrate on anything but the feel of Shiro's warm, muscular and almost comforting weight against his body, and in his arms. *God, he feels good.*

But the idea of having a dick up his ass was just plain scary, even if it was Shiro's. Or maybe *because* it was Shiro's?

"You're thinking too much." Shiro pressed his lips against Rusty's throat, stirring shivers and a soft sigh from Rusty. "Don't think." He spread his knees and pushed, rubbing his cock against Rusty's cock and belly. "Feel."

Rusty's cock stirred, pulsed and filled, curling his toes with anticipation. He groaned. If Shiro kept this up, he was going to cum. He almost smiled. Another wet dream…

Except that he hadn't been *able* to cum. He froze, and the fine hairs on his body lifted. *Uh-oh…* "Shiro, we need to stop! You're making me hard!"

"Oh? You only just noticed that now?" Shiro chuckled. "A little late, don't you think?" He leaned down and nipped at Rusty's nipple.

Rusty yelped and pushed at Shiro's chest. "Damn it! Cut it out! It took me hours to get rid of the last one!"

Shiro smiled and propped his chin on one hand. "Shoveling snow was a clever way to do it, too. I was impressed."

Rusty scowled up at him. "I couldn't get rid of it any other way!"

Shiro chuckled. "Of course not." He reached down and grasped Rusty's firm length. "I have a cock-ring on you." He lowered his head and swept his tongue from the root of Rusty's cock up the length to swirl around the flared crown.

Near-painful delight scorched down Rusty's spine and thrummed in his cock. "Ah!" He sat up and grabbed for Shiro's hair. "What…what are you doing now?"

Shiro tugged his hair free and pressed a palm against Rusty's chest. "What am I doing?" He shoved Rusty flat down among the pillows, and flashed a sharp smile. "What does it look like?" He leaned down and delivered a line of small licks across Rusty's cock-head.

Each tiny lick jolted Rusty in the balls. He threw his head back and gasped. "It feels like you're trying to drive me insane!"

"Good guess." Shiro smiled, showing teeth. "You got it in one." He sucked Rusty into his hot, wet, fanged mouth.

Rusty's hands fisted in the sheets, and his hips jerked in sheer reflex. "You're doing this on purpose!"

Shiro released Rusty's cock with a wet smack and smiled. "Absolutely."

"You shit!" Rusty shot a glare at Shiro and twisted, shoving at Shiro's hand, pressed against his chest. "Cut it out!"

"Be still!" Shiro's gaze narrowed. "My teeth are very sharp." He smiled, exposing the full, pointed length of his fangs. "We don't want any accidents. Do we?"

Rusty froze, staring at the long fangs so very close to his dick. *Shit!*

Shiro smile gentled, hiding his teeth. "Now, lie down and take your punishment, naughty boy."

## ~ *Twelve* ~

*R*USTY FELL BACK AMONG THE PILLOWS.

"That's better." Shiro lowered his head and sucked Rusty's traitorous cock back into his mouth, his tongue lashing across the sensitive underside.

Rusty gasped and twitched with every stroke of Shiro's torturous tongue. He was trapped in a dream with a fox-spirit determined to drive him insane with lust. And it was working, too. *Son of a fucking bitch!* Insidious delight gathered, pooled and tightened. His balls pulsed, so very close to the brutally delicious clench of release…and went no further. A choked cry escaped his lips. "Shiro, please…!"

"Hmm…" Shiro released Rusty from his mouth, raised his head and licked his lips. "There already?" He pulled his hands free and eased back, sitting up on his knees, and smiled. "Good." He wiped his mouth with the back of his fist.

*Oh, come on!* Rusty grabbed for Shiro's shoulders. "Shiro, damn it, finish me!"

"I don't think so." Shiro eased out from under Rusty's hands and stretched out on his belly. He looked at Rusty over his folded arms and smiled. "Unless…" He rolled up onto his side, showing off the long line of his muscular belly and the arching curve of his impressive erection. "You're ready to let me have you?" The tip of his white tail swished across the sheets.

"Uh…" Rusty bit down on his bottom lip. He was so close to cumming. Would it be so bad really, to just let Shiro…fuck him in the ass? Chills ran up Rusty's spine. Yes, yes, it would. He looked away and shook his head. "No."

"No?" Shiro dropped back onto his belly and propped his chin on his palm. "Oh, well, too bad for you." His eyes narrowed to slits of copper fire and his smile tightened. "I told you before, the only way you're getting off is with my dick up your ass."

Rusty bared his teeth and slammed his fist on the mattress. "Bastard!"

"You better believe it!" Shiro bared his fangs and his ears turned back to lay flat against his skull. "You're not getting yours until I get mine!"

Rusty jerked back and shivered in spite of himself, his heart slamming in his chest. He scowled to cover his reaction. "Shit." He flopped back among the pillows and covered his face with his hands. "This isn't a dream. This is a nightmare. Fuck!" he moaned into his palms. He was so damned hard his dick was seeping. Maybe he should just give in and get it over with?

"Why not let me have you?" Shiro leaned close and set his hot palm on Rusty's upper thigh. "I'll make it good for you."

Rusty dropped his hands and snorted. "Had a lot of practice, have you?"

"Enough." Shiro smiled and tilted his head to the side. "Want the details?"

*Details?* Rusty's stared. Did he really want to know about Shiro's sexual experiences? No, no, he didn't. He swallowed and looked away. "I think I'll pass on that one."

Shiro grinned. "What a pity." He rose to sit on his heels, his knees spreading wide to display the arched curve of his cock. "Shall we continue?" Shiro licked his lips and curled his fingers around his cock. "I want to see if your mouth is good for more than just sarcasm."

"What?" Rusty scrambled up onto his knees, his eyes widening. He wanted a blowjob? "You're kidding, right?"

"I've had my mouth on you, it's only fair; don't you think?" Shiro crawled across the mattress toward Rusty. "If you do a good job, I could change my mind about not letting you cum." He lunged.

"Wait a minute!" Rusty gasped and threw himself backwards to the very edge of the round bed.

Shiro crawled after him. "Come on, play nice, Rusty."

Something grabbed the back of Rusty's head, and pulled.

"What the…?" Overbalanced, Rusty tumbled right over the edge of the bed. He landed on his ass hard, and sprawled on the floor. "Ow! shit…" He opened his eyes to darkness. He was back in his workroom on the floor by the side of his futon, fully dressed and painfully erect. "Damn it, I think my ass is bruised." He sat up in a small pool of light cast by the furnace's pilot light and rubbed his butt. The dream was definitely over.

Something big moved among the shadows by the windows. It looked kind of like a person hunched over.

Rusty rose to his feet, staring hard. "Is somebody there?"

The shadow shifted, and straightened to stand upright. "What if there is?" The voice was young, male and sullen.

Rusty's brows shot up. A teenage boy…? "How did you get in here?"

"How did *I* get here?" The figure moved between the windows and the row of sewing machines. "*You* brought me, you moron!"

"Me?" *That voice…* He knew that voice from somewhere, but…? "Do I know you?"

The shadow boy chuckled, but it was a hard, vicious sound. "God, you're such an idiot." He turned to face Rusty in the dark. "You know me, all right." A sliver of pale light form beyond the curtains revealed that his T-shirt was torn, and something was over his face. There was a gleam of gold where the eyes should be and the shadow of tall ears rose past his head. He leaned forward, toward the Singer machine. There was a soft click and the standing lamp went on. "I'm your worst nightmare, asshole."

Rusty winced in the glare, then stared. The kid was a full head and shoulders shorter, scarecrow thin, wearing a ragged, faded and filthy gray T-shirt. Dark red hair spilled in a scraggly mess about his bony shoulders, with unkempt sprays rising past the edges of the pitch-black grinning fox mask that hid his entire face.

*What the fuck...?* Icy shock froze Rusty where he stood, then a white-hot rush of anger made his teeth clench. *That thieving bastard!* He took a step toward the boy and pointed at the kid's face. "Look, I don't care how you got in here, but that's mine, you brat! Give it back!"

The kid released a short laugh, and shook his head. "God, you're so stupid."

Rusty took a stiff step toward the kid. "I said, give that back!"

The kid tilted his head from side to side and spoke in a high-pitched whining falsetto. *"Give that back."* He made a sound of disgust and folded his arms over his scrawny chest. "Why should I? You don't want it!"

Rusty jerked back as though struck. "What kind of bullshit is that? I made it! It's mine."

The kid shoved his hands in his pockets and eased back from Rusty. "So?"

"So?" It took everything Rusty had not to lunge right over the machines. "What's that supposed to mean?"

"It means that you haven't got a snowball's chance in hell of catching me." He turned and dashed along the windows heading for the stairs.

"Get back here!" Rusty bolted after him. "I'm gonna kick your ass!"

"You got to catch my ass first!" The kid grabbed the handrail, taking the stairs in long leaping bounds, giggling...and not in a nice way.

Rusty leapt up the stairs right behind him. Piss on not using his full strength, he was going to put that damned kid's lights out for him.

The kid stopped at the top of the stairs. "Too slow, asshole!" He took a sharp right out the door and into the shop.

At the top of the stairs, Rusty grabbed the doorframe to swing himself around the corner, after the kid. He was nowhere in sight.

Thumping footsteps signaled that the kid was taking the stairs to the upper floor where all the costumes were stored.

Rusty pounded for the stairs. How the hell had that kid gotten up there so fast? Rusty pushed his unusual strength into his strides. Unfortunately he wasn't exactly used to using his full strength when he ran, and crashed into the wall at the base of the stairwell. He pulled himself from the dent in the drywall he'd made with his body. Wiping the chalky plaster from his arms, he groaned at the mess. The owner was going to have his head.

Loud thumps announced that the kid was on the floor above.

Rusty lunged up the staircase, leaping the stairs three and four at a time. There was an exit in the basement, the front door and the kitchen door on the main floor, but the two upper floors didn't have any exits. Where the hell did the kid think he was going up there?

At the top of the stairs, Rusty spotted the kid halfway down the hallway. "Get back here, you little bastard!"

"Make me!" The kid ducked into one of the rooms.

Rusty lunged down the hall, skidding into the room after him. "You brat!"

Giggling hysterically, the kid sidled through the racks of costumes lining the wall pelting to the closed door at far end of the room. He jerked open the door. "Still too slow, old man!" He dashed into the adjoining room.

Rusty followed the kid in and then out of, costume-filled room after costume-filled room, his temper getting shorter by the second. The kid seemed to have an instinct for knowing were all the room-joining doors were.

Rusty swung out the door after him and into the main hallway. "Look, just hand the mask over and I won't break you in half."

"Oh, like you're going to scare me?" The kid turned to the side and jerked the back of his pants down to the top of his bony ass. The view went a little hazy and dark, then became a thick black foxtail attached to the base of the kid's spine and hanging out over the top of his pants. "Now do you get it?"

Rusty groaned. *God, not another damned fox!* No wonder he was so fast. Or was this just another dream? Rusty wiped a hand down his jaw. The hallway looked perfectly clear, and both the beard-stubble under his fingers and the sweat running down his neck didn't feel dream-like, but how could this kid be real? "Did Shiro send you?"

"Che…" The kid turned to face Rusty. "No, stupid, you brought me here, I already told you that!" His tail switched back and forth in clear annoyance.

"Okay, so you're a fox. Great…" He scrubbed a hand through his hair. "What do you want with my mask?"

"I'm not just *a fox*. What do you have in that head of yours, bricks?" The kid snorted. "Here, have a clue, moron." He turned his back to Rusty. The entire center back of the T-shirt was a huge filthy and ragged hole—like the exit hole of a gunshot. The kid turned back around and tugged on the front of his T-shirt. "Notice anything else?"

Rusty stared. There was a hole, the size of a quarter, in the front of the kid's stained shirt, right over his heart. It matched the huge blast hole on the back of the kid's shirt. Ice filled Rusty's veins and his heart hammered painfully. His ears filled with the rush of night wind through autumn leaves.

*You're dying…*

Rusty's knees weakened and he grabbed for the wall. "You're…me?"

"I'm your shadow, you moron. I don't want your mask—I *am* your mask. I'm everything you didn't want to know, everything you couldn't deal with, everything you threw away." The kid pointed at the mask. "All jammed into this stupid thing years ago." He set his hands on his hips. "And just so you know exactly where I stand…" He jabbed a finger toward Rusty. "I hate your fucking guts, too!" The kid bolted for the stairwell at the far end of the hall.

"What?" Rusty dogged the kid's heels all the way up the stairs to the next floor. "What are you talking about? I never hated you." He winced. "Err…me."

The shadow fox looked back from the top of the stairs. "Oh, cut the crap. You wanted to get rid of me so bad, you made this so you could pretend to be normal. So fine, have it your way. I'm leaving! I hope you enjoy the last two weeks of your dumb-ass life!"

Rusty tripped on a step. "Last two weeks…?"

"That's right. Without me to act as your soul, your body is dead meat." The shadow fox set his hand on his hip. "And good riddance."

Rusty held out his hand. "So, give me back my mask!"

"Oh, it's way too late for that. If you want me, you're going to have to catch me!" The shadow fox bolted down the hall.

Rusty pelted after him. The chase continued in and then out of all that floor's rooms, too.

Downstairs, the bell jingled loudly, announcing that someone had come in through the front door. "Rusty, are you in here?" It was Des.

The shadow fox skidded to a halt in the middle of the hall, and turned to face Rusty. "Well now, looks like I get to have some real fun!"

Rusty's heart nearly stopped in his chest. Des didn't stand a chance against the pissed-off fox.

The shadow fox launched himself toward Rusty, aiming for the stairs.

His heart in his mouth, Rusty rushed to cut him off. "You leave her alone!"

The shadow fox slid right under his fingers. "Too slow, dead man!"

Rusty threw himself down the stairs, leaping after him. "Des, get out of the store! Get out now!"

"Rusty?" Des frowned up at him from the bottom of the stairs, dressed in her winter coat and a red wool ski hat. Snow encrusted her jeans to the knees. "What's going on?"

"Des, damn it!" Rusty pounded down the stairs. The entire downstairs was as bright as day. She must have turned all the lights on. The pissed-off fox was nowhere in sight. "I told you to get out!"

Des jerked back as though struck. "What? Why?"

The shadow fox dropped feet-first from the ceiling, landing right behind her. "Hello, pretty."

"What the…?" Startled, Des whirled around to face the kid.

The shadow fox dove headfirst into Des's belly, his entire body disappearing into her body.

Des gasped and staggered, then collapsed to her knees.

Rusty tripped and nearly fell to the floor in sheer shock. "Oh, God…Des?"

Des straightened, then climbed back up onto her feet with her back to Rusty. "Not anymore, butt-wipe!" The voice was male, youthful, and completely unlike Des. She turned to face him. Covering her face was his black fox mask. "Now you're really going to pay for ditching me."

# ~ Thirteen ~

RUSTY STARED AT THE BLACK FOX MASK COVERING DES'S FACE IN ABJECT horror. "Des!" He grabbed for her shoulders.

She dodged to the side and giggled. It wasn't a pretty sound. "Missed me!" The voice was youthful, masculine and frighteningly familiar.

Rusty's heart hammered with rank fear along with his anger. The shadow fox was inside of Des, and controlling her body. He had no clue how to get the fox back out of Des, but he was betting that the mask was the key, which meant he had to get close enough to pull it off her. The problem was, even possessed, she was just a normal kid and he could really hurt her with his unusual strength. "Your fight is with me, not Des, leave her out of this!"

The fox-possessed girl tilted her head to one side. "Do you love her?"

Rusty took a step closer. "Yeah, I love her. She's my friend!"

She shrugged. "I suppose that'll do."

Rusty shook his head in confusion. "What?"

She folded her hands behind her and stepped back. "This would be a lot more interesting if I could possess the one you really love, but I guess she'll do."

"Oh, right…" Rusty snorted. "I'd like to see you try to possess Shiro." He froze in complete shock. Why the hell had he said that? He waved a hand. "Never mind, leave Des alone!"

The shadow fox snorted. "And once again, denial rears its ugly head." She raised a finger. "That's going to be the death of you, you know." She stepped back toward the wall. "Let's see if I can make that happen today!"

Rusty still didn't know if this was real or a dream, but Des was involved. He couldn't take the chance. God only knew what that fox planned to do with her, but he had to do something, and fast. He leaped for the possessed girl. "Get out of her!"

She dodged Rusty's hands. "Make me get out!" She turned and jumped up against the wall, then ran up it and onto the ceiling. Her long, dark braid slid out of her coat collar to dangle toward the floor.

Rusty stared up at the shadow fox using Des's body to stand perfectly at ease on the ceiling overhead as though it were the floor. "Holy shit…" A shiver wracked through him. "Don't hurt her, you bastard!"

The shadow fox tipped her head back presenting her masked face to Rusty. "If I'm a bastard, where do you think it came from, dumbass?"

"What? I'd never hurt Des! She doesn't deserve this!"

The shadow fox pressed a hand to her heart. "Oh? But I do?"

"Oh, come on!" Rusty paced under the possessed girl, his bare heels thumping in frustration. "What did I ever do to you?"

"What do you mean, what did you do?" The possessed girl paced directly above, mimicking Rusty. "You treated me like some disease, like some monster! You hated me enough to lock me away—in this!" She pointed to the mask. "Well, guess what?" She folded her arms over her chest and looked away. "I hate you, too!"

Rusty cringed. The fox had a painfully valid point. He'd made the mask to put an end to the craziness that had infected his life. The unusual strength that had forced him out of school sports, the weird dreams about palaces in clouds, the shadows moving at the corners of his eyes day and night, killing his concentration, and his grades… "I was just a kid in high school when all that weird shit happened." He looked away and tugged at his sweatshirt. "I didn't hate you. I was just…" *Scared.* Scared by all the strange things going on around him, and desperate to forget about a gunshot wound to the heart that hadn't left a mark on him. "I just didn't know how to deal with any of it."

"So you locked me away in the dark, and...forgot about me?" Something slid out from under the mask, dropping onto Rusty's cheek. "That was a shitty way to deal with it."

Rusty wiped at his cheek and his fingers came away moist. *Tears?* He stared up at the pacing girl. The fox was...weeping? Something squeezed around his heart, and it hurt. Maybe blocking out all the weirdness hadn't been the right thing to do. Maybe he could have found a way to deal with it back then. He stared at his wet fingertips. "You're right. Blocking it out was a shitty way to deal with it." He looked up at the possessed girl. "I'm...I'm sorry."

"You're sorry?" She stomped her foot and tilted her back to face Rusty. "Damned right you're sorry!"

"Yes, I'm sorry I messed up, okay? What more do you want from me?" Rusty held out his hands. "Whatever it is, you can have it, just please, don't hurt Des because I messed up." He knew damned well he was begging, but that didn't matter. Not with Des's life on the line.

"What do I want? I want you to suffer the way I suffered!" She bolted across the ceiling, her boot-heels thumping and scuffing the aged white paint.

"Shit!" Rusty pelted after her.

The fox-possessed girl turned into the stairwell and ran up the sharply slanted ceiling, clearly heading to the upper floor.

Rusty leapt up the stairs after her. "Hey! Where are you going?"

"If you can keep up, asshole, you'll find out!" She scurried up the stairwell ceiling past the second floor to the top floor, and then ran down the hallway ceiling.

Rusty tore down the hall after her. Why were they up here? Where the hell did the fox think it was going with Des?

The possessed girl knelt at the small trapdoor to the attic and pried it open. The square of painted plywood fell to the hallway floor.

"Wait!" Rusty skidded on the carpet, halting below the square hole to the attic. An icy breeze brushed his cheeks. "What are you doing? There's nothing up there!"

The fox's masked face appeared in the hole to the attic. "Oh, but there's a lovely view on the roof. Why don't you join me?" She turned away, and disappeared from view.

Rusty frowned. The roof? His heart slammed hard in his chest. The roof was steeply pitched, covered in snow and ice, and four stories from the ground. If Des fell... He hunched down and jumped, grabbing for the edge to the attic. For once, his odd strength was actually useful. He wrestled himself up and through the fairly snug hole. *Hello, square hole, this is round peg...*

The attic was dark, dusty and cramped by the pitch of the roof. The floor was non-existent. Filthy, aged fiberglass filled the spaces between struts. If he stepped on it, his foot would go right through the ceiling below. At the far end, the wind whistled through a small, round and wide-open window.

Rusty scowled. The fox must have taken Des out that way. He stared down at the heavy struts riddled with ancient nails. He was barefoot. Fuck it, he'd heal, and fast.

He ran for the window along one of the struts. His heel landed hard on an exposed nail and agony shot all the way up to his knees. He gasped and fell hard, sprawling across the strut. "Son of a bitch!" Gritting his teeth, Rusty pushed back up and kept going.

He caught a nail on the big toe of his other foot. "Ow, shit!" He teetered, and grabbed for the ceiling strut by his head. He didn't fall, but he gained a sharp cut on the heel of his right hand.

Limping, Rusty finally made it all the way to the far end of the attic. He shoved his head out the open window into falling snow. Four stories straight down, the snow was piled up to the bottom edge of the first story window. Damned deep snow for this area, but that would not be cushion enough if Des fell from the roof.

He turned to look up. The snow covering the house's decorative gingerbread edging showed handprints. She must have gone up from here.

Rusty shoved his shoulders through the window, it was a tight fit. The window was smaller than he'd thought. Halfway out the window, he turned over and grabbed the decorative edging. His hand ached from the cut, and blood smeared the gingerbread. He frowned. That should have healed already.

He scrambled for another handhold and caught the base of the antique TV antennae still nailed to the roof. Very carefully, he pulled himself upward. Icy wind slid up under his clothes while blowing snow blinded him as to what might be up there waiting for him.

Clawing and scrambling for toeholds, Rusty landed belly down in the deep snow on the slanted roof. Breathing hard, he shivered from the sweat fast-freezing under his clothes. He couldn't ever remember being this cold. He wiped the snow from his face and looked for the Des.

Des was sitting on the very center of the roof's longest peak with blown snow swirling all around her. If she fell from there…

*Shit…* Rusty inched his way along the pitched roof to the steep peak that Des was perched on. "Okay, you made your point, fox. I'm seriously freaked out here. You can get down any time now."

The possessed girl tilted her head. "How come you didn't call your boyfriend to come help you get me?"

"You mean Shiro?" Rusty reached the side of the slanted roof and stopped right under Des's feet. The good news was that his hands and feet were too numb to feel any pain. The bad news was that his hands and feet were too numb to be able to feel anything at all. He hoped to God he'd be able to catch her if she slipped. He turned to look up at Des. "Why would I call him? This is between you and me."

"Ah!" The fox held up a finger. "But he's the one that did it to you. He gave you this…this monster."

Rusty's temper snapped. "He did it because I was dying! He was only trying to help!" He froze, shocked by his own words. It was true. Back then, Shiro *had* been trying to help. Shiro had said he loved him… Rusty looked out toward the snow-covered trees. Maybe he'd been looking at everything—what Shiro had done then, what Shiro was doing now, all the wrong way?

Rusty turned back to stare up at Des, balancing on the edge of the roof, just out of hand's reach. "Please, come down. I don't want anybody hurt, not Des, not me and not you, either. I admit I fucked up, I should have tried to learn to live with…all the weirdness."

She leaned over Rusty. "So you finally admit that you're not human?"

Rusty stared at the precariously tipped girl above him. "Yes, I admit it. Even with you in the mask, I was always stronger than I should have been, and…" He winced. "And then there were all the costumes I made." He took a deep breath. "To feed from." It actually hurt to admit it, or was it just from breathing the cold air?

The girl nodded slowly. "For someone who hated my guts, I'm amazed you came up with a way to feed us." She tapped the mask with a finger, then set her hands in her lap. "Not that it did much more than keep us breathing."

Every hair on Rusty's body stood up. She wasn't holding on. "Please put your hands back on the roof."

She tilted forward over Rusty. "Why? Do you think I'll fall?" A large swathe of snow dislodged from the roof's side, and sailed to the distant ground.

Rusty swallowed. "I'd rather not find out."

She folded one hand under her arm and propped her chin on her free hand. "So, you admit that you're not human."

Rusty slapped the side of the roof. "Yes, yes, I said so, didn't I?"

"Wait, I'm not finished! Do you admit that I am in fact your soul—ears, tail and all?"

Rusty swallowed. Did he have a choice? "Yes."

She set her hands on her knees. "Do you want me back?"

Rusty's hands fisted in the snow against the side of the roof. That fox was better off in his body than anyone else's. "Yes."

The possessed girl tilted her head to the side. "Are you sure?" She pointed a finger at Rusty. "You get all of me or nothing, I mean it! I won't go back in here again." She tapped the side of the mask.

"Yes, damn you!" Rusty wanted to hit the side of the roof again, but he just couldn't make his numb hand do it.

"All right, you win. I'm coming back."

Rusty sagged against the roof. "Thank you."

"But…"

Rusty's heart tried to stop in his chest. He looked up at her. "What?"

She opened her arms wide. "You still have to catch me!" Des tipped forward and fell.

*"Don't…"* Rusty threw his arms wide to grab her. Des landed heavily against his chest and Rusty clutched her. Something dark and hot stabbed into his gut, spilling into his blood like boiling pitch. Voices babbled unintelligibly on the edge of his hearing. His brain went fuzzy and his body seemed disconnected, as though he'd just chugged an entire bottle of Jack Daniel's. His knees gave out and pitched backwards.

Rusty shouted in shock. "No!" He was about to die. He'd fucked up again, only this time his mistake was going to cost Des her life, too.

And he would never see Shiro again.

Locked together and blinded by flying snow, they tumbled down the sharply sloped roof, then rolled over the edge, and into open air. They fell.

Eyes closed tight, tears freezing on his cheeks, something hot and hard exploded around Rusty's heart. He shouted in despair. "Shiro!"

# ~ _f_ourteen ~

RUSTY CLUTCHED DES AGAINST HIS HEART AND FROWNED IN CONFUSION. They had rolled off the roof and were falling four stories straight down to their deaths, but it was taking an awfully long time to get to the ground.

Rusty's eyes snapped open. He winced in the glare. It was so bright. Had the sun come out? And since when was sunlight so yellow? With Des cradled against his chest, Rusty passed by the third story window slowly, as if they were falling in slow motion. Golden light glared from the window glass straight into his eyes. Rusty winced and looked down at Des in his arms. Behind the frames of her glasses, her eyes were closed and her cheeks pale. She was obviously unconscious. He supposed that was a good thing, but…

But his hands were blazing like yellow stars, the light burning from under his skin. In fact his arms were glowing right through his sweatshirt. His entire body was glowing. He blinked. *Holy shit!*

And they *were* floating. Well not quite, they were still falling, but at what seemed like a really slow rate. They eased past the second story window. Rusty felt his heart leap. Only one story to go. They *weren't* going to die!

And then the snowy ground rushed up to meet them. Rusty hit the deep snow on his back with a muffled whump and a hard slam. It knocked the wind out of his lungs, making him see stars and his eyes water. He gasped in a breath and groaned. "Oh…shit."

Rusty stared up at the roiling cloudy sky. It had stopped snowing. He took a deep breath and shuddered violently in surprise. He was alive. He was bone-tired, but definitely alive. Flopped on top of him,

Des's heart thumped against his. They were both alive.

Rusty closed his eyes in absolute relief. Cheer filled his heart to the brim and overflowed to drip down his cheeks. He wanted to laugh, but for some reason he was just too damned tired to summon more than a smile. "Des, Des, we made it."

Des didn't move.

"Hey, Des?" Rusty struggled to sit up in the deep snow. "Des?" She flopped across his lap like a rag-doll, her eyes closed, her breathing very slow. Had the scare made her pass out? He tapped her cold cheeks. "Des? Come on hon, wake up."

Des didn't move.

"Oh, shit…" Rusty pulled her up by the shoulders of her coat. "Des, girl, come on, you're scaring me here. Wake up!"

"Rusty, what in hell were you thinking?"

"Ah!" Rusty jumped in surprise and turned.

Shiro scowled down at him. He looked perfectly human and as beautiful as a Renaissance angel. "You scared the hell out of me!"

Rusty's heart flipped over in his chest. He grinned stupidly. God, he was happy to see him. "You came."

Shiro snorted. "Of course I came, once you dropped the damned barrier."

"Huh?" Rusty frowned. What the hell was he talking about?

Shiro dropped to his knees at Rusty's side in the snow and set his palm on Des's dark head. "Isn't this the little girl that works in your shop?"

"Yes, but…" Rusty felt a hard chill and shivered. "She won't wake up."

"Let me see her." Shiro pulled Des from Rusty's lap into his arms. He brushed the hair from her pale brow and set his brow against hers. "She's very deep under." He frowned in concentration "Shit, she's in a coma."

"A…coma?" Rusty's heart tried to stop in his chest. "How…?"

Shiro set his hand over her heart, and then his eyes widened. "My God, her soul has been drained practically dry!"

"Her…what?" Rusty reached for Des. "We have to get her to a hospital."

Shiro turned sharply, pulling Des away from Rusty's reach. "A human hospital can't fix this!" Shiro faced Rusty and bared his teeth in clear fury. "What happened?"

Rusty pushed to his knees. "Me? I… She…" How did you say this? His face flushed with heat. "We fell off the roof."

"I know that, I saw you fall." Shiro's lip curled and his eyes narrowed. "I also saw you using far more power than I gave you to slow the fall. Where did you get it?"

Rusty flinched back. "You saw that?"

Shiro leaned close to Rusty's face and shouted. "What the fuck did you do to her?"

Rusty fell back on his butt. He'd never seen Shiro so angry. "She was possessed…"

Shiro stared at Rusty, and all color left his face. "You possessed her?"

Rusty looked away briefly. His shadow had done it, but his shadow was still a part of him. He ducked his head and looked up at Shiro. "Yes."

Shiro's cheeks flushed with color and his jaw tightened. "Possession is forbidden!"

Rusty closed his arms around himself. "I wasn't exactly in complete control of myself at the time."

"Do you have any idea what you have done?" Shiro rose to his feet, cradling Des. "Possession is worse than rape! It not only takes complete control of the victim's body, it drains the soul to the point of death!"

*Death?* Rusty felt a sharp stab in his heart and shoved upright, teetering on his bare and frozen feet. "I tried to stop it as soon as it happened! But I didn't know how!"

Shiro's eyes narrowed and a growl rumbled low in his chest. "Do you really hate the idea of being my lover that much?"

"What?" Rusty's his heart chilled. Where the hell had that come from? "That doesn't have anything to do with it!"

"Oh, doesn't it? You threw yourself out of my dream, and then stole enough power from this child to not only break my spell, but block me out of your presence. That looks an awful lot like someone trying to avoid me."

Rusty flinched back from Shiro's glare and tipped, falling into the snow, and landing on his butt. "Shiro, that wasn't it at all!"

"I was an irresponsible fool." Shiro turned his back on Rusty shaking his head, his mouth tight. "I didn't think you were even capable of something like this." He scowled and stepped away across the top of the snow, and strode toward the trees. "I should have never..."

"Shiro!" Rusty pushed back onto his feet and tried to follow him. He sank knee-deep into the snow. "Wait! Where are you going?"

Shiro stopped and raised his hand, his fingers wide. "To save this child's life, if it's still possible." He curled his fingers and ripped downward, creating an opening in thin air leading into misty darkness.

"Shiro!" Rusty stumbled in the deep snow. "Take me with you. Please, I want to help!"

Shiro froze, but didn't look back. "Don't you think you've done enough?" He stepped through and the hole sealed itself behind him.

Rusty dropped to his knees in the snow and shuddered. *Shit...* He was still fucking things up. *Des...*

Shivering and in a daze of chest-crushing pain, Rusty stumbled through the snow to the back stairs, and then into the shop. He stripped to the skin right there in the kitchen, leaving his soaked clothes on the floor by the washer, then stumbled into the bathroom for a shower.

He closed his eyes and let the hot water run down his shoulders and back. It scalded the hell out of his skin, but didn't thaw the ice around his heart, or stop the trembling. His hands fisted against the tiles. "Des, please don't...don't die."

Wrapped in nothing but a stained towel, he thumped down to the basement and crawled under the blankets. Sleep came and went. Only a few hours later, he got back up, dressed and went back upstairs to start the coffee.

According to the radio on the kitchen windowsill, the entire city was closed down due to the unusual snow. Everyone was advised to stay off the roads except for emergencies.

Unable to sit still long enough to finish even one cup of coffee, Rusty went to work cleaning up the mess he'd made from the chase through the shop. He straightening all the disturbed costumes on both upper floors, nailed the square of plywood back over the attic access, then tidied the displays on the main floor. He vacuumed the shop from the top floor down. He scrubbed the kitchen floor. He cleaned the bathroom.

And everywhere he went, a memory of Des waited there for him, smiling, laughing or hollering for some kind of assistance from her lazy head costumer… She couldn't be gone.

Exhausted, he went back into the kitchen and refilled his cup, then flopped down on the kitchen chair to stare blankly at the steaming brew.

The phone didn't ring.

The front door didn't jingle.

The radio was the only sound in the whole shop. Rusty sipped his cooling coffee and stared out of the kitchen window. His head began to throb. He set his brow down on his arm, just for a minute…

The phone rang loudly.

"Ah!" Rusty jumped up onto his feet, knocking the old wooden chair to the floor. Outside the kitchen window, red and orange streaked the sky and shadows encroached across the snow. The sun was going down. The digital clock on the coffee machine said 4:43.

The phone rang again.

Who could be calling this late, especially with the whole city shut down from the snow? He stared at the phone mounted on the wall by the back door. What if it was Des's parents? What could he tell them?

The phone rang again.

Rusty flinched. *Better answer it.* He walked to the phone, and fumbled the receiver to his ear with shaking hands. He took a breath. "Costume Company, can I help you?"

"Hey, Rusty?" The voice was youthful and feminine.

Rusty's heart tried to stop in his chest. It sounded like... "Des?"

"Yeah, it's me. Hey, I won't be coming into to work this week...."

"Des!" Rusty's knees shook and he fell back against the door. "Thank God! Are you okay?"

"Oh, yeah, I just came back home from the hospital..."

Rusty frowned. "The hospital?" She was in the hospital?

"It's stupid, really." She chuckled. "They say I passed out from exhaustion."

Rusty scrubbed the back of his head, ruffling his uncombed hair. "You...what?"

"Exhaustion. I know it sounds really dumb, huh? Anyway the emergency people told me that some blond guy brought me to the emergency room, saying that he'd found me passed out in the snow."

*Some blond guy?* Could that have been Shiro? Rusty turned to stare out the kitchen window. Full dark had arrived. "When? When did you get to the hospital?"

"You know that's the funny thing. I know it was still morning when I passed out, but the doctor says that the guy brought me in sometime around two in the afternoon."

*Two?* That meant Shiro must have had her for at least four hours. Rusty turned to stare at the kitchen table. "Are you okay? What did the doctor say?"

"He said there's nothing that a couple of days of rest won't fix. I'm just overtired. He's convinced that it was from too much late-night studying, then walking to work in all that snow this morning. I'm supposed to take a bunch of vitamins, drink lots of orange juice and rest. My mom came and got me, so I'm home now with a doctor's note for the rest of the week. Think you can handle the shop by yourself?"

"Yeah, no problem." Rusty grinned. She was okay. Des was okay.

He hadn't killed her. He wiped at his aching eyes and discovered tears. "Hey, Des?"

"Yeah?"

Rusty took a deep breath. His chest felt so tight that he could barely get the words out. "You're a good kid, you know that?"

Des chuckled. "Don't get all mushy on me, your boyfriend will get jealous."

Rusty sucked in a sharp breath. "Boyfriend?" His voice squeaked only a little.

"Yeah, you know, tall, blond, gorgeous, took you out on a dinner date? That guy."

Rusty swallowed. "Oh, okay." Jeeze, had Shiro's interest been that obvious? He winced. Yeah, it probably had. He waved a hand in nervous dismissal. "Never mind, I'm just glad you're okay."

"Yeah, I'm good, no permanent damage. Don't be too hard on yourself, okay?"

Rusty's smile wavered. "Huh?"

Des sighed. "You know, all that stuff from this morning, the possession thing, then the ceiling and the jump off the roof?"

Rusty's hands shook around the phone. "You remember what happened?"

"Photographic memory, remember? It's why I'm a straight-A student; couldn't forget anything if I tried."

*Oh, my God, she remembers it...* Rusty wiped his hand down his face. "Look, I'm really sorry for all that weird shit..."

"Rusty, it wasn't your fault, not really, and you did try to stop it."

But it was his fault. All of it. Rusty leaned over to ease the ache in his chest. "I'm... I'm just glad you're okay."

"I'm fine, really. Oh, crap, Mom's yelling for me. I got to go. Take care and give your boyfriend a kiss for me, okay?"

Rusty wiped at his eyes. "Okay."

"Bye!"

"Bye." The phone clicked. Rusty hung up the phone in a state of shock. Des was okay, Shiro had been able to help her. He slid down to the floor and sat with his back against the kitchen door. He hadn't killed her. *Thank God.* And she hadn't freaked out over all the weirdness. He shook his head and smiled. Des was a lot stronger than she looked. He would have been seriously freaked.

Rusty rubbed his jaw and frowned. Why hadn't Shiro stopped by to tell him that Des was okay? He climbed to his feet and stared at his now ice-cold cup of coffee sitting on the kitchen table. He'd seriously pissed Shiro off, but just how pissed off was he? Did Shiro never want to see him again? He rubbed at his chest, but the ache was inside, around his heart.

Rusty looked out the kitchen window at the red-tinted sky. It had stopped snowing that morning, about the same time he'd gone off the roof, so the main roads should be plowed and sanded enough to drive. He should go home. He'd have to shovel the car clear, but he was pretty sure he had tire-chains in the trunk.

Rusty headed for the basement to get dressed and collect his shoulder bag. If only his headache would go away.

# ~ *Fifteen* ~

RESSED IN HIS BLACK JEANS, WASHED YET AGAIN, AND THE BLACK turtleneck he'd originally worn to work, Rusty almost felt as though the last two days hadn't happened. But they had. He sighed and stomped into pair of tall and shiny black Santa Claus boots. It was confusing. Everything seemed different, and yet not much had really changed.

Except that his mask was missing.

Rusty rolled his eyes, and pulled on his long black wool overcoat. He must have left it outside in the snow. He winced. He couldn't believe he forgotten about it. Well, he'd been a little distracted by the falling, and then the glowing and then Shiro being mad at him, and Des nearly dying. He sighed and wrapped the red and green Santa's Helper muffler around his neck. He'd go look for it once he got outside. It was black, how hard could it be to find in all that white snow?

He shut off the shop's lights, checked the locks on the front doors, set the security alarm, then walked out the back door, locking it behind him.

Rusty walked over to the impact crater he and Des had left in the snow and looked around for the black fox mask. It was nowhere in sight. He was pretty sure the mask hadn't been on Des's face when they were falling, so it had to have fallen off somewhere. He looked up the side of the building. Maybe it was still on the roof?

Rusty groaned and headed for the Saturn. He was not going to climb back up on that roof again. *Not today, anyway.* He'd done more than his share of roof-climbing for one day. There was always tomorrow.

Determined to ignore the ache in his chest and the mounting headache, he popped open the trunk and pulled out the tire-chains. He set them around his back tires with practiced ease. He grabbed the snow shovel from where he'd left it against the side of the building, and shoveled his four-door Saturn out of the snow. He cleared a pathway to the road in far less time than expected.

He took a last look at the shop just as the first stars of the evening appeared in the twilight sky, and his heart ached. He didn't want to go. Rusty shook his head. He had no reason to stay.

Heaving a sigh, he slogged through the snow back to the parking lot. He left the shovel leaning against the side of the shop, got into his car and drove out of the costume shop's parking lot.

As expected, the main road was fairly clear, though snow was piled high to either side of the road.

Rusty stopped at a small self-serve gas station. After pumping gas, he went into the tiny mini-mart to pay for his gas and grab a soda.

At the checkout, the cute blonde teenage girl behind the counter announced Rusty's purchase total, blinked, then grinned. "Hey, mister, cool contacts!"

Rusty pulled money from his wallet and rolled his eyes. A lot of people assumed that the unusual green of his eyes had to be contacts. "I'm not wearing any."

The girl chuckled, but her smile faltered. "Oh, yeah, right, like normal people have eyes like a cat?"

Rusty handed her the cash. "I'm sorry, but the color is real."

The girl took the money, her mouth twisting in annoyance. "Not the color..." She hit a few buttons on her register. "I'm talking about the shape." She handed him the change. "The middles are up and down like a cat's, not round like a person's."

*Up and down?* Rusty froze, change in hand. His heart thumped in his chest. "Uh, thank you. Can you tell me where your rest rooms are?"

"Against the back wall." The girl waved toward the back, and greeted the next customer in line.

Rusty snatched up his can of soda, turned on his heel and fled to the back of the store.

In the tiny men's room, he stared into the mirror over the battered sink. He blinked in shock. She was right. His pupils had changed shape, from round to tall slits. *What the hell is this?*

A sharp ache stabbed through his temples. Rusty clapped his hands to the sides of his head and felt his ears change shape under his fingers. He looked into the mirror in time to see the points of his ears poke up from his hair, only they were triangular in shape and covered in red fur. *Fur?* He hissed in a breath. *Oh, shit!*

Rusty felt a stabbing pain in his jaw, and winced. In the mirror his teeth lengthened into a double set of upper and lower fangs. Suddenly the back of his skull blazed fiercely. He gasped, nearly biting his lip with his new teeth in the process. The ferocious ache spilled down his spine to boil in his tailbone. He clenched his teeth to stop from crying out and twisted to the side. He braced his elbows against the bathroom wall and watched his fingernails extend into curved black claws.

The pain at the base of his spine increased. He scrabbled to get his jeans unfastened and shoved down past his ass, along with his briefs.

Abruptly, all the pain disappeared.

Panting, Rusty pushed back from the wall. *What the hell...?* He slid his hand under his coat to press against the small of his back. There was a line of sleek hair marching up and down his spine. He slid his hand down and discovered a tail. A big one.

He jerked his coat to the side to look. Attached to the base of his spine at the very crack of his butt cheeks was a rather handsome red foxtail, the exact color of his hair, tipped in snowy white. And it was huge, almost as long as he was tall. It draped all the way to his ankles, curving above the floor for a good foot or so.

Rusty stared. He had a tail. He slid his fingers through the silky fur and carnal pleasure spiraled up his spine. It was real, and soft, too.

He slid his hand down the fur again, and that deliciously sensuous shivery sensation returned. It felt almost…sexual, and vaguely naughty.

He dropped his tail in alarm. *Damn it, I'm petting myself!* He closed his eyes and took a deep breath. *Okay, let's get a grip…* He turned to stare into the mirror at his slitted green eyes and tall red fox ears. He had become a *kitsune*—a fox demon, like Shiro.

And he'd done it in the men's john at a mini-mart.

Get a grip? *Yeah, right!*

He looked at the bathroom door and scowled. He couldn't walk out in public like this! He had to change back. But how?

All the werewolf fiction books had the werewolves willing themselves back into their human forms. It couldn't hurt to try it.

Rusty closed his eyes and focused on what he used to look like. He broke out in a cold sweat and his stomach churned sickeningly, but that was it. *Damn it!* Now what? Tail or no tail, he had to get out of there.

Rusty tugged his jeans and briefs up, but couldn't. The tail was in the way. He groaned. How the hell was he supposed to close his jeans when he couldn't get them up over his butt?

*Shit…* Rusty pulled his jeans and briefs as high as he could. Leaving them open and his dick very nearly exposed, he rolled the top edges down. He pulled his shirt down over his open pants and buttoned his coat closed. Unfortunately, the tail was beyond floor-length. It stuck out well past the calf-length hem of the coat, and there wasn't a damned thing he could do about it.

Rusty reached for the bathroom door, glanced in the mirror, and jerked to a halt. His ears were standing straight up, well past his hair. *Damn it!* He clenched his teeth and willed them to lay down.

They didn't want to.

Annoyance rushed through him, and his ears turned back, dropping. *Oh, that did it!* His mood lifted, and so did his ears. Rusty groaned. The damned things were on autopilot!

If he couldn't make them lay down, then he needed to cover

them. He needed a hat.

Rusty frowned. He was pretty sure his gray Humphrey Bogart fedora was in the Saturn's trunk, but that was out there, and he was in here. He needed to put something over his head to get him to the car. He focused on the green and red stripes of his festive scarf and smiled. "Ah-ha!" He tugged his scarf out from around his neck and put it over his head and ears. He tucked the scarf's ends into his coat and checked the mirror again.

He looked like a bag lady.

He rolled his eyes. *Whatever!* He pushed out of the bathroom and headed for the exit door in a rush. He shoved at the glass door and it flew open. Rusty gasped and snatched for the handle before it could crash against the wall. Apparently he was stronger than before.

Rusty hurried to his Saturn popped and the trunk. He collected his brimmed gray hat, closed the trunk, then rushed over to open his car door. He stared at his bucket seat. How was he supposed to sit, never mind drive, with a tail? Did he have a choice?

He unbuttoned his coat. Glancing over his shoulder, he wrestled his tail to the side, then sat gingerly with his long tail curved along the passenger seat. He closed the car door with a strong sense of relief. He jerked the scarf down and set his hat on his head. His tall ears dropped flat, tucking back under the brim all by themselves. Apparently they didn't like to be covered.

He lifted his chin to look in the rearview mirror. Not bad. Not perfect either, but it was better than the bag-lady look, and he had his peripheral vision back. Now all he had to do was drive.

He put his key in the ignition. With a bit of wriggling, and leaning a little to the side, he was able to press the clutch pedal and handle the stick-shift, though it wasn't anything close to comfortable. Sitting on his tail ached all the way up his spine. Grimly, he stepped on the clutch, started the Saturn and put the car in gear. He licked his lips and rolled away from the gas pump and out of the parking lot.

Tire chains jingling, Rusty drove the Saturn up the snowy street. What the hell was he supposed to do about looking like this? He might be able to manage work, his job was in a costume shop, after all. But what about other stuff, like cashing his paycheck or buying groceries? "Pardon me, ma'am, don't mind the tail." He rolled his eyes. *Oh, yeah, right...*

Carefully he ran his tongue along his brand-new fangs, and pricked his tongue. He flinched. Eating was going to be an interesting challenge. He shook his head. No way in hell he could live like this. He had to change back.

Shiro slipped from shape to shape, so there had to be a way to do it. Rusty winced. He really didn't want to face Shiro, especially not like this, but he didn't have any other options. Rusty turned the wheel and headed for the historic courtesan district and the Oriental Playhouse. It was the only place he knew to look for him.

The massive wooden doors of the huge gate marking the historic district were wide open. Rusty passed through the gate at a crawl, his tire chains ringing against the snow-covered cobbles. The main street had been plowed fairly clear, with huge mounds of snow piled up against the sides of the tightly packed buildings. The shop doors, sitting only inches from the main thoroughfare, were brightly lit with round red and black paper lanterns. People bundled for the cold were everywhere. Snow or not, the historic district was open for business, and business was apparently appreciative.

Rusty eased into the winding and narrow backstreets. They weren't quite as clear as the main street, but he could still get through. On instinct alone, he found the second and older gate arching over the road.

Rusty stared at the wide-open oak and cast iron doors within the tall red posts of the gate. The old courtesan district was open, though the lanterns on these shops were smaller, and further apart. The walking crowds were thinner here, but still managed to keep his movements to a crawl.

After only a small navigation struggle between a few snowdrifts and some drunk pedestrians, Rusty somehow wandered into a narrow drive jammed between several old buildings and found the hidden parking lot Shiro had used. At least, he was pretty sure it was the same parking lot. The buildings in this district looked a lot alike.

Rusty parked and released a deep breath. He'd made it. But he had to walk the rest of the way—with a visible tail. Not that he had a choice.

Rusty got out, closed his door and stepped away from his Saturn, his boots crunching in the snow. His tail was long enough to sweep the ground, however, touching the ground was something his tail apparently had no intention of doing. It refused to stay down and the back of his coat was split, so a good two feet of the big red fluffy thing curved upward.

Rusty groaned and kept walking. He really didn't have a choice.

"Hey, mister, you've got a tail!" The voice was masculine, and slurred.

Rusty stiffened. *Oh, shit...* He kept walking.

"Hey, mister! I'm talking to you!"

Rusty cringed. *Fuck...* He stopped and turned to face two rather large middle-aged guys in green-gray hooded parkas. They leaned against each other with flushed cheeks and dazed gazes. They were obviously drunk.

Rusty peered carefully from under the brim of his hat. "Can I help you?" *Can they see my ears?*

The one on the left curled his lip aggressively, showing bad teeth. "So, what's with the tail?"

The one on the right could barely hold his eyes open, and drooled a little. "Tail..."

Rusty tried not to flinch back from the sour-milk stench of their beer breath. What to say? Oh, wait, he had the perfect excuse. He smiled. "I work for a costume shop." Rusty reached to his coat and tugged out his wallet. He pulled out a business card and held it out to them. "Here."

The belligerent drunk guy on the left took it and stared blearily at it. "Oh, okay." He smiled. "Good job, that tail looks almost real."

Rusty snorted slightly. *I'll just bet it does.* He waved. "Thank you, but I'm in a hurry."

The drunk guy on the left nodded. "Okay." He waved the card. "Thanks!" He and his companion tottered off.

Rusty heaved a sigh of relief. *That fixes that problem.* He hurried down the narrow street. Now all he had to do was figure out how to do the same effect, should someone come to the shop and actually ask for the damned costume.

# ~ Sixteen ~

AFTER PASSING OUT BUSINESS CARDS TO A FEW MORE DRUNK GUYS, RUSTY finally found the quiet back streets; the ones empty of pedestrians.

Twenty minutes later, shivering with cold, Rusty finally stopped before a tiny alley that no one had bothered to shovel clear. There wasn't even a footpath in the snow. Rusty turned all the way around in the narrow lane. The wood-walled, tile roofed buildings were all identical, and dark. Not one lantern was lit in any doorway. The soft glow from the snow was the only illumination.

He had no idea where he was. Rusty pulled off his hat and scraped his fingers across the top of his head and through his hair. "Damn it, Shiro, where in hell are you?" His hair flopped into his face, brushing his cheeks to fall past his chin. He frowned. He didn't remember his hair being that long.

He ran his fingers through his hair again, pulling it forward over his shoulder. It fell in a red mass almost past his heart. He swallowed. It *was* longer, a *lot* longer and a brighter red, too. He could actually make out the color in the night-dark alley.

"Looking for someone, pretty boy?"

Rusty whirled, his fingers clenching the brim of his gray hat.

A black-haired man in a long black coat leaned back against the building with one knee bent, his foot propped against the wall. He casually lit a cigarette with a silver lighter.

The lighter's flame exposed blue highlights gleaming in the unrelieved blackness of his hair. He wore it combed straight back from the deep peak of his brow, and it flowed down to his waist in a spill of ink. Midnight-dark eyes peered at Rusty from under straight black brows. Sharp cheekbones and a strong jaw-line defined his aggressively masculine, winter-pale face. His supporting foot didn't leave a mark in the snow.

Rusty's ears dropped to the sides of his skull and the hair on his spine rose, from the back of his neck all the way down to the tip of his tail. He had no idea what this guy was, but he knew in his bones that he was not human.

The guy's lighter snapped off and he blew smoke. He chuckled softly. "Didn't mean to scare you."

Rusty took a deep breath and let it out slowly. No need to freak out. With his unusual strength, he could handle just about any kind of trouble that came his way. "You just surprised me, that's all."

"I see." The guy walked away from the wall, his steps leaving no trace in the snow. He turned to face Rusty. Strands of his pitch-black hair lifted on the slight breeze. "You're new. I can tell."

Rusty decided to let that comment pass. "If you'll excuse me, I'm looking for a friend of mine. He works in this district."

"Is that so?" The guy's lips curved in a slight smile. "Well, how about me? I work in this district, too. Will I do for a friend?"

Rusty stared. *What the...? Oh...* He snorted, then smiled tightly. Apparently this guy thought he was looking for an escort. "Thanks, but no thanks. I have enough problems with the one friend I already have."

"Really?" The guy tilted his head to the side and gestured with his cigarette. "You know, you really shouldn't walk around like that."

Rusty blinked. "Like...what?" The tip of his tail twitched. Heat filled his cheeks and he rolled his eyes. "Oh, the tail and stuff." He sighed. "I still haven't quite got control of changing back yet."

The guy's smile broadened. "That new, huh?" He tossed the cigarette to the side. "Good." He took a leisurely step toward Rusty.

Alarm seared up Rusty's spine, making his heart pound. He backed away. "Seriously, I already have a friend, I don't need another one."

"I heard you." The guy shook his head and tall black ears parted his inky hair. "But that friend isn't here now." A pitch-black foxtail eased out from under the hem of his coat. "And I am."

Rusty froze. *Another fox?*

The black fox took another step toward Rusty and smiled, showing long teeth. "Don't worry, I'll take very good care of you."

Anger seared white hot down Rusty's spine, making his tail straighten and his ears flatten to his skull. "Try it and die, you pushy bastard."

The black fox eased closer, gliding across the top of the snow. "You really think you can stop someone like me?"

Rusty bared his long teeth, dropped his hat, and raised his hands, showing his claws. "I don't give a shit who—or what—the hell you are…" His voice came out deeper than expected, and a low rumble boiled in his chest. "What part of 'I already have a lover' aren't you getting?"

The guy stopped two body-lengths away. His chin lifted and his eyes narrowed to slits, but his smile remained.

"What a lovely thing to hear coming out of your mouth." The amused masculine voice was very familiar, and right behind Rusty.

Rusty spun around.

Shiro smiled from only an arm's length away. "Causing trouble again?"

Profound relief slammed Rusty right in the gut. He grabbed Shiro by the upper arms. "Why the hell didn't you come back?"

Shiro crossed his arms and his brow lifted. "Are you saying you missed me?"

Rusty jerked his hands from Shiro's arms and opened his mouth to deny it, to say that he hadn't missed him at all. The lie stuck in his throat and wouldn't come out. He ducked his head and glanced away. "Yeah."

Shiro snorted with clear sarcasm. "How sweet."

Rusty flinched and his ears lowered. Shiro was still pissed at him.

The black fox cleared his throat. "So, this is *your* pet, Shiro-

*sama?*"

Shiro lifted his chin, focusing past Rusty's shoulder. He sighed and rolled his eyes. "I'm afraid so, Koji-*san.*"

Rusty turned around to scowl at the black fox. He was once again in human guise, leaning against the wall of the building, calmly smoking a cigarette. Rusty glanced at Shiro. "You know this guy?"

Shiro chuckled. "Of course. Koji-*san* is one of us, though something of a...specialist in fixing disturbances."

Rusty frowned. "He's a cop?"

Koji shrugged and looked away, waving his cigarette. "More like clean-up and repair."

Rusty ground his teeth. "Then if you're supposed to be taking care of problems, why the hell were you harassing me?"

Koji rolled onto his side to lean against his shoulder, giving Rusty a level stare. "Because your little snowstorm is on my to-do list."

Rusty stiffened. "What? I didn't make all this snow! I don't know anything about magic!"

Shiro set his hand on Rusty's shoulder and turned Rusty to face him. "I told you, just being in this world is enough to make things happen."

Rusty shook his head. "But I've never done anything like this before."

"You never had this much power before, either." Shiro raised a brow and delivered a tight smile. "I fed you, remember? Apparently it was just enough to awaken one of your dormant abilities: weather working."

Koji chuckled. "Let me guess, this is his first transformation, too?"

"Among other things." Shiro's gaze narrowed and his mouth thinned into a severe line. "Rusty-*kun* here has had a very busy day."

Rusty hunched his shoulders and dropped his gaze. Yeah, one fuck-up right after the other. He felt his tail actually curl under him. "Thank you for taking care of Des."

Shiro patted Rusty's shoulder and his smile returned, though his eyes remained narrow slits. "Don't worry, I'll punish you thoroughly for your transgressions."

Rusty jerked upright, stepping back. "What?"

Shiro tilted his head. "Don't you think you deserve punishment?"

Rusty felt his cheeks warm, and turned to the side. He had hurt Des. He did deserve to be punished. He crossed his arms. "I...understand."

Shiro nodded. "Good."

Rusty winced. *Jeez... Rub it in, why don't you?*

Koji blew cigarette smoke and snorted. "Need any help with that punishment?"

Shiro's lifted his gaze and focused on Koji. His ears tilted back and his eyes narrowed, though his slight smile remained. "I believe I can manage."

Rusty's cheeks burned.

Koji's eyes widened. "Ah, okay." He raised his hand to cover his smile. "Pity."

Shiro set his hands on Rusty's shoulders, forcing Rusty to stand facing him. "Are you ready to leave here and come with me?"

*Leave?* Rusty stiffened and tightened his arms around himself. "I, uh..." His fingers dug in. His nails bit though his coat sleeves and cut into his arms. He flinched and pulled his hands away. His long nails were pitch black, curved and pointed. They were claws, something ordinary people didn't have.

Ordinary people didn't have fangs, claws or tails. Ordinary people didn't change the weather or possess other people. Ordinary people didn't feed on the souls of others. No matter how hard he'd worked to deny it, he wasn't an ordinary person. He tucked his hands under his arms and stared at the toes of his boots. Shiro had been right all along. He didn't belong here. He released a breath. "Yeah, I guess so."

"Excellent." Shiro gripped Rusty's shoulders and turned him toward the snowy alley. "Koji-*san*, if you wouldn't mind, could you open the door?"

Koji stepped away from the wall he'd been leaning against, and tossed away his half-gone cigarette. "You worried he'll bolt on you?"

Shiro's nails bit into Rusty's shoulders. "It wouldn't be the first time."

Koji's brows lifted and he smiled. "Oh, is that how it is?"

Shiro snorted. "You have no idea."

Rusty hunched his shoulders and a growl escaped. "Hey! I'm right here, you know."

Shiro growled right back. "And it only took how many years to get you here?"

Rusty curled his lip. "Okay, fine, you made your point already!"

"Years? Ouch!" Koji winced dramatically. "No wonder he's such a mess." He turned his back to them. "Okay let's get you home." He clapped his hands together loudly, then pulled them apart. Between his palms the world parted, revealing a swirling gray and misty void. The void broadened, arching upward and outward into a round hole large enough for two people to step through. Koji turned to them and smiled. "Your door, Shiro-*sama*."

Shiro shoved at Rusty's shoulders. "Go."

Rusty nearly tripped in the semi-deep snow. "I'm going! I'm going already! Give me a freaking break!"

They passed Koji and the black fox grinned at Shiro. "Have fun."

Shiro smiled very broadly, showing all his teeth. "I intend to."

Rusty stiffened. "What is that supposed to mean?"

"Never mind." Shiro pushed him toward the hole in the world. "Keep moving."

Koji laughed and shook his head.

*Bastard!* Rusty stepped into the misty grayness, wondering if he'd just made a humongous mistake.

# ~ Seventeen ~

PALE MIST SWIRLED, OBSCURING THE SKY AND ANYTHING ELSE THAT MIGHT be around them. It wasn't dark, but the fog was too thick to see anything that wasn't within an arm's length. Rusty was pretty sure he was walking on grass, but he couldn't see his feet to be sure. And it was warm, far too warm for winter. It felt like late spring.

Rusty wiped the back of his hand across his dripping brow. It was far too warm for the heavy wool coat he was wearing, not to mention that the coat rubbed against his tail just wrong, and his feet were killing him. He' been sure he'd chosen the right size of boots, but his toes felt painfully cramped.

Shiro's hand tightened on his shoulder. "Rusty, it's a bit warm for that coat, don't you think?"

"Yeah, I kind of noticed that." Rusty tugged at his buttons. It was going to be a pain to carry, but if he wore it too much longer, he was going to pass out from overheating. He undid the last button and opened the coat. The top of his pants were rolled down past his hips. Fully half his butt was hanging out the back, and his short curls were clearly visible in the front. He'd pulled his shirt down over the top of his pants, but the shirt had climbed up above his navel. "Shit." He clutched the coat closed. "I can't."

"If you don't, you'll pass out from heat exhaustion once we get to the lake." Shiro sounded distinctly amused.

Rusty turned to frown at him. "Wouldn't a lake make the air cooler?"

Shiro smiled. "Absolutely, if the lake wasn't close to boiling in temperature."

Rusty blinked. "A hot lake?"

Shiro curled his fingers around Rusty's coat lapels. "Think of it as being a gigantic hot spring, with islands." He tugged, opening Rusty's coat, and blinked. "Ah, so that's how you solved the problem of wearing trousers with a tail."

His cheeks heating furiously, Rusty jerked his coat closed. "I couldn't come up with anything else."

Shiro tugged at Rusty's coat lapels. "Relax, no one will see you, at least not until we get to the island."

Rusty refused to let his coat go. "We're going to an island?"

"Yes, my house is on an island. You'll find it quite comfortable." He raised his brow. "Rusty, take off the coat."

Rusty groaned. "Fine." He shrugged out of his coat.

Shiro snatched it out of his hands. "Thank you."

"Hey!" Rusty grabbed after it.

Shiro looped his arm around Rusty's waist, and twitched the coat out of his reach, catching him against his chest. He dropped the coat. It vanished in the mist.

Rusty jerked in Shiro's embrace. "My coat!"

"Calm down, you won't need it."

Rusty scowled up at Shiro. "Need it or not, that coat was mine."

Shiro looped both arms around Rusty, holding him close. "Need it or not, it would have disappeared the moment it left your hands. It doesn't belong in this world."

Rusty stared up at him. "You're shitting me."

Shiro snorted. "Afraid not." He raised his hand and absently ran his fingers through the thick red mane that Rusty's hair had become. "Things that don't belong in it tend to disintegrate."

Rusty swallowed. "Even people?"

Shiro smiled sadly. "If left here too long, yes, even people."

Rusty looked away. That was just plain scary.

Shiro caught Rusty's chin and focused his copper gaze on Rusty. "You belong here, Rusty. Believe me, you belong." He leaned down, pressing a kiss to Rusty's lips.

Feeling in need of some form of reassurance, Rusty didn't even think about turning away. He closed his eyes and parted his lips to taste Shiro's kiss. He still couldn't get over how good Shiro tasted. He smelled good, too; warm male and something else, something wild.

Shiro deepened the kiss, sucking on Rusty's tongue, and slid his hands down Rusty's hair, then down his back in a caress.

Rusty groaned in appreciation. A shiver lifted the fine hairs all down his spine and warmth pooled low, spilling into his dick.

Shiro's caressing fingers reached the hem of Rusty's shirt, caught hold, and tugged upward, hard. Rusty's shirt slid up his body, then off his arms faster than he could grab for it. Shiro tossed the shirt away, and it disappeared just as the coat had.

"Damn it, Shiro!" Rusty crossed his arms over his bare chest and scowled. "I am not stripping naked!" Not when he was more than half hard just from the kiss.

Shiro smiled. "That won't be necessary, at least not right now. However..." He looked down at Rusty's feet. "Those boots are probably quite uncomfortable."

Rusty looked away. Shiro was right; the boots were pinching his toes all to hell. He was close to limping. He rolled his eyes. "Fine, whatever..." He lifted a foot and grabbed the heel of his boot. He tugged at it and fell over. He landed on his butt in the grass, pinching his tail. He yelped.

The fog was too thick to see Shiro's face, but Rusty could hear his chuckles just fine.

Rusty shoved his red tail out of the way and pulled the boot from his foot. In a fit of annoyance, he threw it into the mist. He grabbed for his other boot, and frowned. Under his sock, his foot seemed...weirdly shaped. Curious, he pulled off his sock. His foot was longer, and bonier than he remembered. His toes were longer, too, and they were clawed, just like his fingers. Panicked, and not quite sure why, he tugged off the other boot, and the other sock. His breath caught. His feet matched, but they didn't look like...his feet. They didn't look like human feet at all. He swallowed. "I want my body back."

Shiro squatted in front of him, setting his elbows on his knees. "Rusty, you've made your transformation. This is your body now."

Rusty stared up at Shiro's human face. "But you can change."

Shiro slowly shook his head. "My human semblance is just that, a semblance." The mist swirled around Shiro's body and he went slightly out of focus. "It's merely an illusion that disguises my actual form." The mist parted, and pointed white ears lifted from his silver hair. His clothes had become layers of white, blue and then pale gray ground-sweeping robes, tied closed with a broad silver sash. The pale gray sleeveless over-robe was heavily embroidered with stylized white feathers. A thick, silver foxtail curled around his feet. "This is my true form." He nodded at Rusty. "And that is yours."

Rusty shivered. "You're saying that I can't go back?" His voice trembled, just a little. His red tail curled close around him and he clutched it, not thinking about what he was doing. "This is...permanent?" He was going to look this way for the rest of his life?

Shiro stood up, rolled his eyes. "All right, fine, I'll say it." He folded his arms across his chest. "You make an incredibly handsome red fox, and I admit to wanting to see you without your shirt."

Rusty blinked. That wasn't quite what he'd expected, but strangely it was enough. He left his boot and his socks on the nearly invisible grass, rolled forward onto his feet, and brushed off his knees. "I uh..." He shrugged. "Thank you."

Shiro smiled. "You're welcome." He raised his clawed hand. "Shall we continue? I believe the boat is already at the shore."

Rusty started walking in the direction Shiro indicated. "How can you tell? I can't see a damned thing in this fog."

Shiro chuckled and stepped up to walk beside Rusty. "You'll get used to it." He set his arm around Rusty's bare shoulder. "Eventually."

# ~ Eighteen ~

STARK NAKED, RUSTY STOOD IN THE MIDDLE OF HIS SPACIOUS AND EMPTY room, bathed in the afternoon sun pouring through the wide-open doors, utterly and painfully embarrassed. "Do I get to wear some clothes now?"

Shiro, magnificent in layer after layer of silver and white robes, circled. His gaze narrowed, focusing on Rusty's naked body, and his erection. A slight smile lifted the corner of his mouth. "You'll be dressed soon."

Rusty clenched his jaw. *Bastard...* He'd known that taking his pants off that first night had been a bad idea, but they were just too uncomfortable to sleep in. The following morning, the not-quite-human attendant delivering the breakfast tray politely but firmly declined to bring Rusty a robe, or any other sort of clothing.

Rusty had been forced to keep the bedsheet wrapped around his hips for the past two days. Needless to say, exploring anything beyond the empty room he occupied was right out. He'd pretty much occupied himself by sleeping and eating the meals brought to him.

This morning, however, had been the morning from hell. While eating breakfast, three attendants had rolled up the thick, round mattress, the room's only feature, and shoved it in a closet in the long cedar wall. Without the mattress, there was nothing to sit on but the hardwood floor. Then they'd demanded his bedsheet, for cleaning.

No amount of arguing worked. They weren't leaving without the bedsheet. He'd finally turned his back to them and handed it over, with his tail embarrassingly low and tucked between his ankles.

All of it, from the refusal of a robe to putting his bed away and taking the bedsheet, was by the master's orders. The master, of course, being Shiro.

Heat filled Rusty's cheeks. "You're still mad at me."

Shiro folded his silver and white robes close, then knelt gracefully directly in front of Rusty. "Absolutely." He stretched out a deep green silk cord between the span of his hands. The tasseled ends draped to the floor. "Move your hands out of the way."

Rusty winced and folded his arms across his chest. His tall ears drooped a bit. After two whole days of having ears that moved, he still couldn't quite control them. His tail's movements were a total mystery. He looked down at the top of Shiro's head. "Is that why I haven't seen you since we got here?"

"Not at all." Shiro doubled the finger-width silk cord, leaned close and passed it around Rusty's waist. "You needed time to recover from your transformation." He put the tasseled ends through the loop made by the rope's fold and pulled it snug around Rusty's hips. "I used that time to put a number of duties and affairs in order."

"Oh…" Well, he *had* pretty much slept the past two days away. Rusty frowned. "So, what's with the rope?"

"This is you to wear under your clothes." Shiro made a snug and fairly complicated overhand knot just below Rusty's navel. "I'm sure you'll find it quite…entertaining."

Rusty stiffened. "Entertaining?"

"Or at the very least, diverting." Shiro pulled the cord down to the very top of Rusty's painfully aroused cock. He marked the place with his fingers. "Spread your legs a little wider, please."

Rusty opened his legs, standing with his feet shoulder-width apart. "How long am I supposed to wear this?"

"Through dinner." He looked up and smiled. "And bedtime." He made a very complicated and perfectly round knot.

That meant, several hours. *Great.* He hadn't seen Shiro since the boat ride, and when he did finally get to see him, it involved some kind of kinky bondage. Somehow, it figured. "Is this my punishment?"

Shiro separated the cords, framed Rusty's cock and marked the place on the underside of Rusty's dick. "Part of it." He pulled the cords forward, and made another complicated round knot.

Rusty sucked on his bottom lip. "Couldn't you just...punch me, or something?"

"Punch you? Certainly not!" Shiro smiled broadly showing his long teeth. "That would be over far too quick." He grasped Rusty's cock firmly.

Rusty gasped. Shiro's hand felt cool around his dick, and wonderful. It jumped in Shiro's palm.

Shiro chuckled. "Eager?"

Rusty swallowed. He was desperate, actually. He'd had this stupid hard-on since his first night alone in the big empty room. "I thought you said I broke this stupid cock-ring spell of yours?"

"I didn't exactly take you in hand to check at the time." Shiro slid Rusty's cock between the cords and the two knots. "I must say, I am quite happy to see it still in place."

"Yeah, I bet." Rusty didn't quite groan. The cords framing his dick were snug, but not exactly uncomfortable. However, they were making him painfully aware of his erection.

Shiro pulled the rope up between Rusty's butt-cheeks, past the base of his tail. "Hold this, please."

Rusty reached behind him and pressed two fingers against the rope at the base of his spine. Sunlight poured through the huge and wide-open sliding doors in front of him. This high up the sky was a brilliant blue. Beyond the balcony's railing, he could just make out the tops of the clouds of mist that hid the hot sea far below.

Shiro rose to his feet and walked around and behind Rusty, his robes whispering on the hardwood floor. He took the rope from Rusty's hand and knelt behind him. Shiro pushed Rusty's tail to the left and pressed the rope to the base of his balls.

Rusty gasped. Shiro touching his tail felt good. It felt too good. Rusty's dick quivered, and liquid eased from the tip of his cock-head.

He very nearly moaned. Damn it, he needed a distraction. "So, how come you didn't tell me you were a prince?" He'd been shocked to the core when Shiro's 'house' had appeared through the mists way up high, as though floating on the clouds. Painted in every color imaginable, the monstrous palace occupied the top of a mountain with balconies and hanging gardens all along the cliff heights.

Shiro lifted the ropes to either side of Rusty's tail. "I'm not a prince. I am merely a territorial governor."

Rusty shivered slightly. What Shiro was doing, plus brushing lightly against Rusty's tail, was making it really hard to form a coherent thought. "I don't see much of a difference; you live in a freaking palace with servants."

"My people are staff, not servants. Most of them are secretaries and accountants." Shiro passed the cords under the one encircling his hips and began making a knot just above the base of his tail.

The pressure on Rusty's dick and tail increased slightly. Rusty's tail abruptly arched from the base and twitched sharply from side to side. It had been doing that a lot lately, and he hadn't been able to do a damned thing to stop it. "Hey, can I ask you a question?"

"You may ask." Shiro slid his fingers down the cords and under, pressing slightly on the carefully placed knots.

Rusty bit back an embarrassing groan. The pleasure from Shiro's touch was unbearably exciting. He had to take a breath before he could speak. "My um, tail has been acting...weird."

"You mean the way it moves to one side?"

Rusty licked his lips. "Yeah, it's like it won't stay put."

"That's because you're aroused." Shiro chuckled softly. "Your tail is offering your butt."

Every thought in Rusty's head came to a screeching halt, and heat flooded into his cheeks. "You're kidding, right?"

"Not at all." Shiro rose and walked around him. "By the way, this dinner is a formal engagement with about thirty guests. I expect you to be on your best behavior."

"I'm going to be like this...?" He twisted around and pointed at his twitching tail. "In front of thirty people?"

"Not counting the staff, yes." Shiro rose to his feet and walked all the way around Rusty, clearly inspecting his handiwork.

*Oh, my God...* Rusty couldn't breathe for a full second. He was going to be in a room with thirty people that would all know his dick was hard. "I think I'll skip dinner."

Shiro's stopped directly in front of Rusty and glared. "Absolutely not! You cannot bow out of the bachelor's presentation feast."

"The...what?"

Shiro's chin lifted and he crossed his arms. "Our formal announcement that we are ready for marriage."

*Marriage?* Rusty felt the smile tug at his mouth. "Uh, Shiro, I don't know if you noticed, but we're both male. We can't have kids together."

"Of course not." Shiro rolled his eyes. "You're my consort, not my wife."

*Not his wife?* Rusty blinked. For some reason, that statement actually hurt. "You have a wife?"

"Not yet." Shiro shrugged. "Without a passionate and healthy consort, the ladies won't even consider me."

Rusty frowned. "They want you to have a consort?" The women didn't get jealous? "I don't get it."

Shiro chuckled. "Paired Kitsune need a human-born Kitsune to have healthy children."

Rusty swallowed. "You're saying that we both sleep with...your wife?"

"Our wife." Shiro's ears flicked forward, then one tilted back. "You don't like girls?"

Rusty jerked back. "Of course I like girls!" He folded his arms and scowled. "I prefer them, actually. You are the only guy I've..." He looked away and his ears dropped. "The only guy I've ever had any interest in." There, he'd finally admitted it.

Shiro chuckled. "Good."

Rusty wiped his hands down his face. "This is the weirdest

conversation..."

Shiro grinned. "You'll get used to it."

Rusty shook his head. "Says you."

Shiro stepped behind Rusty. "Your ability to survive on your own is sure to impress the ladies." Shiro slid his fingers up under Rusty's waist-length mane. "And they are going to love this dark red hair."

Rusty trembled. Shiro's fingers felt so good.

"But you're still a bit on the scrawny side."

"Scrawny!"

"Your spirit is severely underfed." Shiro slid a finger down the line of red fur that trailed down Rusty's spine to the base of his tail, drawing shudders. "You'll need plenty of time in bed to build your strength up for the Summer Festival."

*Time in bed...* Rusty's cock throbbed, and his knees weakened. He made a desperate grab for his last escaping thought. "What's the Summer Festival?"

Shiro leaned over Rusty's shoulder and smiled, clearly pleased about something. "That's when the unattached ladies come out in full force to inspect the season's unattached bachelors. With you at my side, we're sure to attract a wealthy and powerful wife."

*A wife?* That meant children, eventually. He wasn't against kids, he just hadn't considered himself daddy material. He cleared his throat. "I don't know if I'm ready to get married and have kids right away..."

"Don't worry, I won't let them rush you into anything you're not ready for." Shiro slid his palms down Rusty's arms. "Marriages don't take place until the Winter Festival." He reached down and stroked a finger along Rusty's cock.

Rusty choked and his heart slammed in his chest. His tail abruptly decided to arch clean over to one side. Blushing hotly, Rusty glanced away. *Stupid tail...* "You're evil, you know that?"

Shiro smiled. "Kitsune *are* considered demons."

"Is that supposed to make me feel better?"

"Does it?"

Rusty clenched his teeth. "No."

"Good." Shiro stepped back and clapped his hands loudly. "Let's get you dressed for dinner, shall we?"

# ~ *Nineteen* ~

*R*USTY LOOKED OUT THE OPEN DOOR TO THE BALCONY OVERLOOKING THE far distant water. The sky was dark, with a thick haze of stars. It had taken all damned day to get him dressed for 'dinner'. He'd been scrubbed, brushed, trimmed and polished within an inch of his life.

It had taken three attendants just to carry his clothes into the room, and then three more to get the multiple layers of split-skirted robes, sashes, beads, buttons and baubles onto his body and arranged. He had to be wearing nearly his own weight in red, orange, black, and green silk, and yet just a few tugs on his sashes and he'd be naked again. Even his over-long red hair, arranged into a loose and decorative tail around an amazingly complicated hairpin, was designed to come down with one tug. It was like he'd been dressed to be undressed.

Rusty winced. Knowing Shiro, that was probably true.

He stepped out onto the balcony. His floor-length forest green over flaming orange robes whispered across the floor with his thick red tail, freshly brushed, waving behind him. He was barefoot, but for the first time in three days, his feet didn't click when he walked. He'd been given a full pedicure and a manicure.

He leaned against the railing and opened his hands to stare at the rounded tips of his once sharp claws. They'd been filed down practically to nubs and polished to a gleam; his toe claws, too. It was kind of unsettling to see them so...blunt. Well, at least he wouldn't rip his clothes accidentally. The bed sheet he'd worn had been full of small tears.

Shiro stepped out onto the balcony with a whisper of heavy silk.

127

"Are you ready?" He leaned over Rusty's left shoulder to look. "Is something wrong?"

Rusty closed his hands. "No, not wrong, just...weird."

Shiro pressed a palm to Rusty's shoulder, urging him to turn and look at him. "Weird in what way?"

Rusty shrugged. "This is going to sound stupid, but..." He opened his hands to look at his blunted claws. "But I feel like I've been declawed to protect the furniture." He tried to smile, but it was surprisingly hard.

Shiro smiled. "Technically that's not far from the truth. Claws are notoriously bad on fabrics." He held up his hand, revealing that his thumb and first two fingers were quite blunt, while the last two fingers were long and obviously sharp. "Once you gain a bit more control over your new body, you'll get to keep the last two."

Rusty shook his head. "I only had the damned things for a couple of days, it shouldn't feel this...weird."

Shiro set his hands on Rusty's shoulders. "It's not weird, it's instinct. You're a fox, a hunter. It makes perfect sense to regret the loss of a primary weapon." He leaned back to look over Rusty's outfit. "By the way, you look quite magnificent. That bright flame under the dark green really suits your hair and eyes."

Rusty stared at Shiro's magnificent blue and silver feather-patterned robes over trailing sheer frost white. Shiro's white mane tumbled down his back, ornamented with tiny braids and iridescent gems. His layered sleeves practically touched the ground.

Who the hell was he kidding? He looked exactly like the prince he insisted he wasn't. Rusty looked away. "Ha, I'll never look as good as you."

"Thank you." Shiro raised Rusty's chin with a finger. "But I disagree." He leaned close.

Rusty lifted his chin, anticipating a kiss.

Shiro pressed his cheek to his and ran his palms along Rusty's orange sash, knotted decoratively over his broader black sash. Rusty felt a strong stab of disappointment.

Shiro's lips brushed his ear. "I see they took care to avoid putting pressure on your rope."

Rusty winced. *That damned rope.* His cheeks were still burning from the staff's sly smiles while they dressed him.

Shiro leaned back, frowning. "Are they pinching?"

Rusty shook his head. "No, not pinching." But in no way, shape, or manner were they comfortable, either. He'd never been so violently hard for so long in his life, even counting the past few days under Shiro's spell.

Shiro plucked at Rusty's collar and fingered the sheer red under-robe beneath the green and orange. "Ah, I figured they'd put you in red."

Rusty frowned. "Is that supposed to mean something?"

Shiro set his arm around Rusty's waist, urging him back into the room. "Red stands for your virginity."

Rusty choked. "But I'm not...!"

"But you are." Shiro slid open the door leading to the inner hallway and grinned. "Though not for long."

Rusty stepped into the hall and winced. "Fine, rub it in, why don't you?"

Shiro caught Rusty's chin and smiled. "Oh, I intend to. I fully intend to rub it in."

Rusty stared at Shiro's lips, so close to his, and his heart thumped in his chest.

Shiro released Rusty's chin, stepped back and held out his right hand, indicating the hallway stretching before them. "Shall we go?"

Rusty felt another stab of disappointment. "Yeah, sure." *Damn it...*

The palace seemed to be nothing more than a maze of soaring hallways bordered by towering, ornately carved red columns. Silk paintings stretched across the walls between little wall-nooks set with decorative tables displaying ornate statuary. Monstrous painted and gilded vases holding gigantic flowers framed the occasional blank wall and every cross-hallway entrance.

Walking at Shiro's left elbow, Rusty stared in growing horror. As decorative as it was, it all looked very much alike. There was absolutely no way in hell he'd ever figure out his way around. Left by himself, he'd be lost in seconds. He had no idea how the staff knew to get anywhere.

But what really spooked Rusty was that he had yet to see a single door; only endless, over-decorated hallways.

Shiro took a sudden turn, and stopped before a pair of heavily carved red doors.

Rusty blinked. "Oh, so there *are* doors in here."

Shiro chuckled. "Many, many doors, but most of them are hidden from casual view." He raised his palm. "It makes it difficult for thievery."

Rusty snorted. "Hell, I'm surprised they don't just get lost. There's so much stuff, it all looks the same. You turn one corner and you don't know where you are."

Shiro lowered his hand. "Did you notice all the rather large flower arrangements?"

"You mean the huge flowers in the big vases?"

Shiro nodded. "They are the key to finding your way around. Once you know what flower is associated with your destination, you merely follow the flowers at the turns."

*Follow the flowers?* Rusty blinked. "That is so...sneaky!"

Shiro smiled and shrugged. "Actually it's pretty traditional." He raised his palm. "Shall we continue?"

Rusty grinned. "Lead on!"

The massive doors opened before them, revealing yet more hallways, only these were crammed with foot traffic in every shape, size, and color. Some human-like, some animal-like, some semi-transparent and floating and some he simply could not identify. There was no mistaking that he was not in the world he had come from.

Rusty tried not to stare, he really did, but it was very difficult. He bumped his elbow against Shiro's and pitched his voice low. "My, you sure have a lot of...people here."

Shiro chuckled. "Most of these are guests, or members of their staff." His voice dropped to barely above a whisper. "They came to take a look at you."

Rusty glanced up at Shiro. "Me?"

Shiro smiled tightly. "I made you when I was young, if you remember. Because I never brought you back with me, they didn't exactly believe me when I told them I had a consort."

Rusty frowned. "They called you a liar?"

Shiro shrugged and glanced away. "I wouldn't go quite that far."

*They'd called Shiro a liar.* For some reason, it pissed Rusty off. He shook his head. "You may be a pain in the ass, but you have never been a liar."

Shiro smiled tightly. "I was a child. Children are notorious for making things up."

Rusty caught Shiro's sleeve, stopping him. "You don't."

Shiro snorted. "You're one to talk. It took quite a bit of convincing to get you here."

Rusty's cheeks heated and he glanced away. "Yeah, I know, but..." He suddenly grinned up at Shiro. "It's not your fault that I'm hard-headed."

Shiro rolled his eyes. "Oh, is that it?" He patted Rusty's fingers on his sleeve. "Shall we continue? I think we've let everyone stare long enough."

Rusty nodded and followed Shiro down the crowded hall. "I hope it's not too much further." He glanced at Shiro. "It's getting really uncomfortable to walk."

Shiro glanced at him. "Are your clothes binding you?"

Rusty's cheeks filled with heat. "No, not my clothes." The damned rope around his dick and balls; it was rubbing. Not in a painful way, but as though a hand was clasped around him, massaging him with every step. The changing scenery had distracted him for a bit, but it was fast getting to the point where no amount of distraction was going to work. He was only seconds away from demanding that Shiro shove him against a wall and do him, just to let him cum.

"Over here." Shiro caught Rusty's sleeve and led him between two huge vases of bright orange flowers. Before a blank wall painted a pale yellow, he leaned close and pressed his nose behind Rusty's right ear. "Ah, you are close to the edge."

Rusty stared up into Shiro's amused copper gaze. "You could say that." He knew well and good that desperation was written all over his face, but he really didn't give a damn. A sudden sharp stab radiated from the scars on the left side of his neck. Rusty gasped, and clasped his hand to his throat. His fingers came away with a slight smear of blood. "Shit."

Shiro's brows lifted. "You're bleeding?"

He looked up at Shiro. "If we don't do something fast, I'm going to stain these clothes."

Shiro smiled and fire seemed to ignite in the depths of his eyes. "Let it bleed. Let it stain. I want them to see you bleeding, for me."

Rusty snorted, and a sour smile lifted the corner of his mouth. "Planning to show me off, are you?"

Shiro grinned, showing all his long teeth. "Damned straight."

Rusty folded his arms and raised a brow, delivering his best cocky look. "Sounds good to me. Let's do it."

Shiro laughed, then shook his head. "I love you."

Rusty stared up at Shiro and his throat went tight. "I...I love you too, you know."

Shiro stilled and the center of his eyes widened. "Do you?"

Rusty could barely breathe past the tightness in his throat, but he held Shiro's gaze. "Yeah." He turned away and folded his arms. "Ah, jeez, now I feel all weird again."

"Rusty?"

"Yeah?" Rusty turned.

Shiro grabbed Rusty, pinning him against his chest in a hard embrace, and slammed his mouth over Rusty's.

Rusty moaned shamelessly. Shiro's kiss erased every thought in his head but the feel of Shiro's body, firm and strong against his, and the taste of Shiro on his tongue. Rusty grabbed onto Shiro's shoulders and kissed him back just as hard. He kissed him, not from hunger or need, but from something else; something that made his heart ache in his chest and his eyes burn.

The kiss ended with them panting against each other's shoulders.

Rusty felt a warm trickling against the left side of his neck. "Ah, shit." He pulled back and smiled sourly. "You got a tissue?"

Shiro grinned. "Why, did you cum?"

"Does blood count?" Rusty poked a finger at his scars and stared at the scarlet running down his fingers. They weren't seeping. They were definitely bleeding.

Shiro chuckled and. "No, but it does give us an excuse to make our appearance short." He reached out to stroke two fingers against Rusty's throat. "I can't have you passing out from blood-loss." He stared at his red-stained fingers, then licked them.

The sight of Shiro's tongue stroking those long slender fingers made Rusty's knees wobble.

Shiro grabbed Rusty's shoulder. "You okay?"

Rusty nodded shakily. "Just don't do *that* again."

Shiro frowned. "Do what?"

Rusty shook his head and pushed back. "Never mind!"

Shiro smiled slyly, and turned to face the wall. "Ready?"

Rusty rolled his eyes. "Fine, let's get this over and done with."

Shiro chuckled. "My thoughts exactly." He knocked on the plain yellow wall. Under his knuckles the wall rippled like water, then shimmered into a pair of massive double doors filigreed with leafy vines in gold set with trumpet blooms of silver.

Rusty shivered. *Magic.* He wasn't sure if he'd ever get use to seeing it, but it was proving awfully convenient. He peeked up at the vase bordering the doorway next to him. The brim was very nearly at eye-level. The pot was indeed full of the same trumpet flowers, though these were an eye-searing orange rather than silver. He nodded absently. *Cool.*

The massive doors opened outward, revealing music and light.

# ~ *Twenty* ~

RUSTY STOOD NEXT TO SHIRO UNDER THE OPEN NIGHT SKY AT THE END OF one of many arching bridges leading from the surrounding palace to what looked like a huge round gazebo. Below them, the steaming sea whispered beneath its veil of mist.

Broad red pillars entwined with golden vines with silver trumpet flowers supported an ornately vaulted ceiling under a gold-plated domed roof. Light and cheerful music drifted out into the night.

Within the gazebo, a gigantic circular cloth-covered table, completely hollow in the center and open at one end, occupied the very center. Low, cushioned stools were positioned all around the table's outer edge. Attendants in bright orange knee-length robes over loose pants busily processed in and out of the table's hollow center, setting out steaming trays piled high with exotic foods.

Rusty felt his heart leap into his throat. There were a lot of people in ornate robes of every description and color wandering around the huge table. He leaned close to Shiro. "I thought you said that this dinner was only for thirty people? That doesn't look like thirty people." It looked closer to a hundred.

Shiro smiled. "I also said, 'not counting the staff. Most of the guests brought their own staff, in addition to traveling companions."

Rusty groaned, just a little. "Terrific."

Shiro caught Rusty's sleeve. "Rusty, do you trust me?"

*Huh?* Rusty's train of thought came to a crashing halt. *Trust...?* He looked up at Shiro.

Shiro's expression was smoothed into pleasant lines and his ears were up, indicating that he was asking a casual question, but the corners of his mouth were tipped down and his gaze was just a bit too focused.

Rusty bit back his flippant, negative answer. This question was more important than it looked. He considered everything that had happened, and everything Shiro had done. A lot of it had been underhanded, but none of it had been to hurt him. He nodded. "I do."

Shiro blinked, then his ears came up and a magnificent smile bloomed. "You're sure?"

Rusty nodded firmly. "Yeah."

"All right." Shiro lifted his chin. "Give me your hands."

Rusty dropped his chin and felt his ears fold back. The tip of his tail switched against his ankles. "What, are you going to tie me up?"

Shiro held his gaze. "Yes."

Rusty groaned. "Ah, jeez, first my dick and now my hands. What is it with you and bondage?" He scowled, but he stuck out his hands.

Shiro turned Rusty's hands palm down and pressed the thumbs together, side by side. "Believe it or not, this is actually traditional." A shimmer of gold appeared around Rusty's thumbs, becoming a pair of broad gold cuffs fused together. "A consort agrees to have their hands bound to show that they trust their lord or lady with their lives." He released Rusty's hands.

Rusty winced. *More magic...* He lifted his hands. The cuffs were actually quite pretty, decorated with the same trumpet flower design he'd seen on the door. He made fists and tried to pull his hands apart. Damned things were strong, too.

Shiro lifted his chin. "Now for the rules."

Rusty's head came up. "Rules?"

"Rules." Shiro dropped an arm across Rusty's shoulder and urged him onto the arching bridge. "Eat nothing and drink nothing that does not come directly from my hand."

Rusty winced. "Isn't that a little extreme?"

Shiro smiled. "Technically it's to keep you from accidentally eating something that will make you ill, but as I am a public official…" He shrugged. "Someone might find it amusing to drug you with something just to embarrass me."

Rusty actually felt a growl boil up. *Freaking petty politicians…* "No eating or drinking anything you don't give me. Got it."

Shiro nodded. "Next, don't speak directly to anyone. If they speak directly to you, nod and smile. If you must say something, tell it to me and I'll say it."

Rusty stopped still. "I can't talk to anybody?"

Shiro ducked down to catch his eye. "Public official, remember? They can and will use anything you say against me."

Rusty groaned. "This is going to be the pits, I can tell." He scowled up at Shiro. "Anything else?"

"Yes." Shiro smiled. "Don't lose your temper."

Rusty's ears pressed back against his skull. "What? Do you think I'm going to start a food fight or something?"

Shiro lifted his head and chuckled. "Let's just say that I know my guests, and I know how insanely protective you can be." He raised a brow. "Up to and including a certain roof-dive?"

Rusty jerked to a halt. "Hey, I didn't go off that roof on purpose, you know!"

Shiro sighed. "Oh, really? I was convinced you were trying to save a certain little girl from your angry spirit."

*What…?* Rusty stilled and his ears lifted. "You know…all of it?"

Shiro gently pressed Rusty forward. "When I was restoring her soul, I got a peek into her memories. She pretty much showed me what really happened." He aimed a glare at Rusty. "While I do not agree with your fox's behavior, he did have every right to be angry with you. You should not have sealed him away."

Rusty's shoulders drooped, along with his ears and tail. "I know."

"Hey, it's done." Shiro tightened his arm, pulling Rusty close. "Don't worry, you'll be thoroughly punished for your misdeeds, I promise."

Rusty groaned and dragged his feet. "Oh, that makes me feel so much better."

Shiro chuckled softly. Suddenly they were standing at the end of the bridge between yet another pair of huge flower vases, in the midst of the mild and colorful pandemonium under the golden dome.

Shiro nudged Rusty around the circular table past people of every conceivable description, not one of them human. They passed a pair of the guests resting on the edge of the balcony that *looked* human, but had huge black-feathered wings and orange eyes ringed in black. Another pair of guests, sipping from shimmering glass goblets at the edge of the table, had shimmering scales and pearls woven into their long, pale hair. The bulk of the guests, however, were foxes dressed in brilliant, ornate robes. A great number of them were frost white, with a few midnight black foxes on the outskirts and an occasional ghost-gray.

Rusty frowned. Was he the only red fox?

One of the more youthful white foxes spotted them and tapped his gray companion with his folded fan. They scooped up goblets and wandered in their direction.

Shiro stopped at a pair of place settings, each with a single orange trumpet flower lying across the clear glass plates. He pulled out a stool and eyed the approaching foxes. "Have a seat. I have a feeling the evening is about to become tedious."

Rusty gripped his long robes as best he could with his pinned hands. His tail conveniently lifted to let him sit, then curled neatly around his ankles. Apparently it was on its best behavior.

The youthful white fox and his sleek gray companion bowed to Shiro.

Shiro nodded in return. "Ambassadors." He eased directly behind Rusty, setting his hands on Rusty's shoulders.

Rusty pasted a smile on his face, and was actually glad Shiro stood directly behind him. He did not like the narrow-eyed look on the white fox's boyishly handsome face.

The white fox lifted his fan and smiled behind it. "Ah, Shiro-*sama*, so the myth of the red fox proves true after all."

Shiro's fingers dug into Rusty's shoulders. "As you well know, most myths have some basis in fact."

Rusty felt his temper spark. *Snotty bastard...* He glared, but somehow he kept his mouth shut.

"Please ignore my companion." The gray fox folded his arms and snorted. "He has yet to acquire a consort willing to remain with him."

Rusty's smile returned. *Why am I not surprised?*

The white fox lifted his chin and his ears tilted back, broadcasting his annoyance.

The gray fox smiled. "I, on the other hand, am surprised you'd let anyone see him at all. I wouldn't have." He winked at Rusty and raised his glass in a salute. "He really is uncommonly handsome."

Rusty's cheeks heated under the compliment.

Shiro chuckled with real pleasure in his voice. "Ambassador, if you only knew what kind of trouble he is capable of causing..." He leaned over Rusty's shoulder as though sharing a secret. "It is true, you know—what they say about redheads."

*What?* Rusty turned to glare up at Shiro.

"Is that so?" The gray fox folded his hands behind him. "Temperamental?"

Shiro smiled down at Rusty. "Tempestuous."

Rusty rolled his eyes. *Oh, please...*

The gray fox laughed gently, and his gaze narrowed. "And yet he bleeds for you."

"Indeed." The white fox's gaze focused on the side of Rusty's throat. "That is quite a show of desire."

Shiro smiled. "His nature is very passionate."

Rusty's cheeks warmed. *Passionate?* He turned away, his ears turning back. *Pricks...* His bleeding wasn't from desire. It was because his spirit wanted Shiro to feed him. He closed his eyes briefly. *With sex.* He sighed. Okay, so maybe it was desire.

Shiro plucked at Rusty's robes, tugging at the collar of his red robe. "Oh, my, I'm afraid he's soaked even his under-robes."

The white fox blinked. "You have him wearing the red?"

Shiro shrugged. "My staff, I'm afraid. They insisted on

traditional."

"Traditional? Oh, then he really is…untouched?" The white fox lifted his fan and smiled behind it, but his gaze showed hot interest. "How very…charming."

The gray fox smiled at Shiro. "I somehow doubt he'll be wearing red for long."

Rusty felt a growl rise and squashed it, but his ears dropped flat to his skull. *Leave my so-called virginity out of this, damn you!*

The white fox tittered. It was not a nice sound. "Oh, dear, I think you've upset him."

Shiro patted Rusty's shoulder. "He's a little sensitive about having waited all this time for me."

*Waited for you? My ass!* Rusty eased his foot back and slammed his heel onto the top of Shiro's foot.

Shiro stiffened and shot a glare down at Rusty.

Rusty gave him his best innocent smile, ears up and everything.

The white fox tilted his head to the side. "Is something wrong, Shiro-*sama*?"

Shiro smiled and dug his fingers into Rusty's shoulders. His last two finger claws pierced the fabric and the flesh beneath it. "Nothing I can't handle."

The sharp pain in his shoulders made Rusty suck in a breath. He leaned forward and twisted just a hair to dislodge the claws. *Bastard…*

The gray fox chuckled. "I see what you mean about his temperament, Shiro-*sama*."

"Oh, yes, never a dull moment with this one." The cheer in Shiro's voice was only a little strained.

They gray fox bowed to Shiro. "I wish you luck with him."

Shiro nodded and shot a tight smile at Rusty. "Thank you, I believe I'm going to need it."

The gray fox lifted his empty goblet toward the white fox. "Ambassador, shall we go refill our goblets?"

"An excellent idea, Ambassador." The white fox bowed to Shiro.

"A pleasure, Shiro-*sama*."

Shiro nodded with a tight smile. "As always."

The two foxes wandered off.

Rusty turned away to glare at the flower on his plate. He would have folded his arms, if his thumbs hadn't been locked together. *So, I'm a passionate troublemaker?*

Shiro took the seat to Rusty's left. "Don't pout. It's unbecoming in a man your age." He turned away and filled a clear glass goblet with a bubbling golden liquid.

Rusty took the opportunity to stick his tongue out at him.

Shiro turned back with the goblet lifted. "Thirsty?"

Rusty eyed the goblet. "As long as it's not alcoholic."

Shiro smiled. "It's ginger ale." He offered the goblet.

Rusty sipped. It was ginger ale, all right.

Shiro took the goblet back, and smiled. "Good boy."

Rusty's cheeks warmed. Suddenly he felt like a two-year old that couldn't handle his own cup.

Shiro picked up a pair of slender sticks and proceeded to pile food on his plate, leaving Rusty's plate holding only the flower. He leaned close. "Don't take anything I just said to those ambassadors to heart. I did not want them to entertain the idea that you might be worth stealing away from me."

"Stealing me?" Rusty rolled his eyes. "Oh, please, like I'd go anywhere with either of them?"

Shiro snorted. "You'd be surprised. Both of them are notorious for 'borrowing consorts'."

"Borrowing...? Wait a minute!" Rusty frowned. "You mean kidnapping?"

"Oh, yes." Shiro smiled sourly. "And they both have a nasty case of 'diplomatic immunity' too."

"Terrific." Rusty shifted in his seat, trying to find a vaguely comfortable position. Sitting put pressure on the rope binding him, especially on that one knot right behind his balls. The urge to cum was a constant ache, making it impossible to concentrate on anything.

Shiro speared a bit of nearly unidentifiable food and offered it. "Don't try to chew it, your fangs won't let you. Just swallow it."

Rusty grimaced. "I kind of figured that out over breakfast that first morning."

Shiro smiled. "Good, then open up and eat. I'm hungry, too."

Rusty took the bite and swallowed. Eating without chewing was still a little weird, but he was getting used to it. Not that he had a choice.

Shiro passed Rusty bits off his plate and spoke to the foxes that stopped by, obviously to inspect Rusty. Some showed mild distain or outright disappointment, while others offered Shiro compliments on his fine catch. The rest of the guests seemed only mildly curious, and more interested in talking politics.

Rusty ate and tried not to fidget in his seat. The wetness seeping from his throbbing dick and slicking his thighs let him know in no uncertain terms that his dick was not pleased with sitting.

Shiro leaned close. "How are you feeling?"

Rusty winced. "Like my dick is going to explode." He immediately ducked his head. He hadn't meant to actually say that out loud.

Shiro smiled. "Oh, really?" He picked up his goblet with his left hand while dropping his right hand under the table.

Rusty felt a warm hand sweep across his lap, brushing the very top of his erection. He hissed and grabbed the wrist with both hands, pinning it to his knee, then turned to stare at Shiro. "This better be you."

Shiro smiled behind his goblet. "Just relax and pretend nothing is happening." He leaned close and whispered into Rusty's ear. "I'm going to remove my spell." He gently twisted his hand free.

Rusty stilled, shocked. Shiro was going to let him cum? "Right now?"

Shiro leaned very close and his tongue swept along the outer curve of Rusty's ear. "Do you want to cum or don't you?"

Rusty shivered and his heart pounded. He did, he really, really did want to cum, but there were over a hundred people sitting all around them; some of them looking right at them. "Right here?" His voice came out breathless.

"I think you can handle it." Shiro breathed into his ear, while his hand slid under the edge of Rusty's robes. "Just try not to moan too loudly." Shiro's warm fingers closed around Rusty's painfully rigid cock. "Oh, you *are* ready."

Rusty couldn't say a word. The only thing he could hear was his own heartbeat, and the only thought in his head was that a hand was on his achingly hard cock, and he was going to be allowed to cum.

# ~ 𝒯wenty-𝒪ne ~

𝒰NDER THE TABLE, SHIRO'S HAND WAS CLOSED TIGHT AROUND RUSTY'S cock.

It felt so good, Rusty shuddered and his eyes watered. He leaned to the side, resting against Shiro's shoulder, and took a trembling breath. "You realize I'll probably shoot off really fast?"

Shiro chuckled softly. "I'm counting on it." He pulled, stroking Rusty's cock firmly but slowly.

Rusty felt something release at the base of his balls, and then boiling urgency seared through him. He could cum, in fact, he was going to cum, and soon. He bit back a moan and closed his eyes so he wouldn't see the people around the table staring at him.

"Rusty, look at me."

Rusty turned to look at Shiro, barely able to keep his eyes open, never mind focused. God, Shiro was so beautiful.

"That's the expression I've been waiting to see." Shiro smiled. "Naked lust." His hand stroked down, slowly.

Delight burned from the base of his spine all the way down his tail, curling it at his feet. He hissed in a deep breath to keep from moaning and grabbed onto Shiro's robes with both hands.

"Hmmm…" Shiro leaned closer and caught Rusty's chin with his other hand. He turned Rusty's head away from the table, forcing Rusty to turn all the way to the side, facing him. "You're bleeding quite a bit."

Rusty winced. "Yeah, I noticed." He could feel blood trickling down his arm and cooling on his chest. His clothes were soaked to the skin.

"Ready?" Shiro gave three quick, hard pulls on Rusty's cock.

Climax slammed violently up Rusty's spine, and his back arched. It felt so good, it actually hurt. His breath caught in his throat and he choked. Pleasure streamed up his pulsing cock, spilling his release into Shiro's palm. He released a small, whimpering groan and collapsed against Shiro's shoulder, gasping for breath. Black spots wavered in his vision. *Shit...* He'd very nearly passed out.

Shiro sighed against his ear. "Very nice." He reached for a napkin and subtly wiped his palm below the table's edge. "Feel better?"

Rusty had to take a breath to speak. "Much, thank you." If only he could see straight.

Shiro chuckled. "You're welcome." He tucked Rusty's robes back into place. "Can you walk?"

Rusty thought about it, and pushed up onto his feet. *Okay...* He took a step away from the table and his knees buckled.

Shiro caught Rusty in his arms before he could topple onto the floor and chuckled. "I'll take that as a no, you can't walk."

Several of the guest rose from their seats, voicing concern.

Shiro turned toward his guests and waved a hand. "No need for alarm." He leaned over, slid his arm under Rusty's knees and lifted, scooping him up like a child, tail and all.

Rusty grabbed onto Shiro's robes with his pinned hands, and cringed. "You're embarrassing the shit out of me."

"Live with it." Shiro turned to face the table with Rusty cradled in his arms. "It seems that my consort is unable to continue, so I'm afraid we must leave you. However, the entertainments will continue as planned."

Rusty snorted against Shiro's shoulder. "You conniving bastard, you set me up."

Shiro turned to whisper against Rusty's ear. "Was that a complaint?"

"Hell, no." Rusty wanted to laugh, but he was just too damned tired. "Get me out of here."

Shiro dropped a kiss on Rusty's brow. "Your wish is my

command." He stepped away from the table and headed toward one of the many bridges arching from the gazebo.

Behind them, laughter erupted from the guests, punctuated by enthusiastic applause.

Rusty groaned. "What the hell is all that for?"

Shiro smiled. "They all know where you're going next."

Rusty already knew what Shiro was going to say, but he asked anyway. "Where's that?"

Shiro chuckled. "To bed, of course."

Rusty kept his mouth shut. His dick was already getting hard.

A door closed.

Rusty snapped awake, still held in Shiro's warm embrace. He must have fallen asleep. He glanced around and discovered that Shiro had carried him into a huge round room with pale gold walls and a domed ceiling supported by pillars of pale cream marble veined in gold. Fully half of the back wall was floor to ceiling shuttered windows, all of which were open to reveal a curving balcony and the night beyond.

Dominating the room's center was a monstrous round dome-canopied bed draped with white silk and sheer gold curtains. The blankets had been drawn back, revealing white sheets and two large pillows.

Rusty swallowed. "Your bed, I'm guessing?"

Shiro released Rusty's legs, letting him stand. "Our bed." He caught Rusty's chin, forcing him to look into his eyes. "Yours and mine."

"Uh…" Rusty took a breath, and released it. "Okay."

Shiro focused on Rusty's lips and leaned close. He brushed his lips against Rusty's in a light kiss.

Rusty raised his chin and opened his mouth to taste that excruciatingly delicious flavor all over Shiro's tongue and lips. His partial erection became a full, raging hard-on.

Shiro buried his left hand in Rusty's hair and tugged at the ornament. His hair tumbled free from its tail, spilling down Rusty's back.

Rusty moaned under Shiro's kiss. He could taste the building fire, but it wasn't enough. He needed more. He needed Shiro to cum. He reached down with his bound hands and searched for the part in Shiro's layered robes. He slid his hands between the layers until he found Shiro's cock. He grasped the hot, rigid length with both hands.

Shiro shuddered and knotted his fingers in Rusty's hair. He tugged, pulling Rusty's head back, breaking the kiss and exposing his throat. "Let go."

Rusty hissed through his teeth. Shiro's fingers were a little tight in his hair. "Why?"

Shiro smiled. "Do you really want me to take you right now?"

Rusty swallowed, and released Shiro's cock with a twinge of sincere regret. "Ah, no." His tail, however, chose to arch over to the side in clear invitation. He winced. *Stupid tail...*

Shiro glanced at Rusty's tail. Chuckling, he set his right hand on Rusty's shoulder. "You seemed to be having mixed feelings." His fingers slid across Rusty's collarbone and eased under the robe's edge. His palm slid downward over Rusty's chest and captured the nipple between two fingers. He plucked.

Delight pulsed in Rusty's nipple and the tip of his dick. He groaned and licked his lips. "Can I have my head back, or at least my hands?"

"Patience, love." Shiro slowly eased Rusty's blood-soaked silk over to the side, baring his chest. "All in good time." He leaned down and sucked at Rusty's exposed nipple.

Voluptuous excitement pulsed in Rusty's nipple and echoed in his cock. He gasped and arched his back, trembling.

Shiro pushed the left side of Rusty's robe down his arm, baring his blood-smeared shoulder. Holding Rusty firmly by the hair, he pressed his lips to the bleeding wounds on Rusty's throat and delivered a long, hot lick.

Shivers spilled down Rusty's body. He gasped and his knees tried to buckle. "Oh, shit…" He grabbed Shiro's sash with his pinned hands, and a small whimper escaped.

Shiro wrapped his other arm tight around Rusty, cupping Rusty's ass in his palm. He sealed his mouth over the wounds in Rusty's throat, and sucked, hard.

A violent bolt of red hunger burned down his spine and slammed into his cock. Rusty shouted. Beyond any thought but the urgent need for release, Rusty straddled Shiro's knee and pressed, rubbing his aching cock against Shiro's hip, moaning greedily.

Shiro chuckled against Rusty's throat. "Oh, no, you don't." He released Rusty and stepped back.

Rusty shuddered out of his haze of lust and growled in frustration. *Damn it!* He looked up at Shiro, ears back, though his knees shook under him. "What?"

Shiro folded his arms across his chest. "Are you ready to give yourself to me?"

*Give myself…?* Rusty blinked in confusion, then understanding crashed over him. Was he ready to take a dick up his ass?

He stared at Shiro's determined and somewhat urgent expression, and sucked on his bottom lip. He knew damned well that sex with Shiro was going to happen eventually. They loved each other, perhaps not in the ordinary romantic fashion, but it was still love. Sex was unavoidable. He fidgeted just a little. His dick was violently, painfully hard. *Ah, hell…* Rusty fisted his bound hands. He looked up from under his hair. "Is it going to hurt?" He winced. *I sound pathetic.*

Shiro delivered a breathtaking smile. "I will take great care to prepare you."

Rusty took in a deep breath and released it. "Okay, I'm…" He took another breath. "I'll do it."

Shiro stepped close and placed a gentle kiss on Rusty's brow.

A strange sense of relief spilled through Rusty. He'd agreed. The fight was over. He sighed and held up his bound hands. "So, what do

I do?"

"What do you do?" Shiro tugged at one of the silk cords binding Rusty's sashes. "I'll let you know when we get there." The cord unknotted and whispered free. He tugged at the knot to the slender orange sash that bound the broad black sash.

Rusty watched the unraveling of his orange sash and his heart pounded in his throat.

Shiro put both arms around Rusty and tugged at the black sash's complicated knot at the center of Rusty's back. "Afraid?"

"Of you?" Rusty felt a strong tug from around his waist. He winced just a little. "No." He wasn't afraid of Shiro, he liked Shiro. He really did want to touch—and be touched—by him. No one had ever made his temper fly or his body burn the way Shiro did. No one had ever made him feel so…alive.

Shiro breathed against his ear. "Good."

Rusty shivered. The loud whisper of silk announced the fall of his broad black sash to the floor. His robes fell open and draped around his feet. He clenched his hands tight and tried to keep from shaking. He wasn't afraid of Shiro. It was being fucked up the ass that had him tied up in knots.

Shiro slid his hands under Rusty's robes and around his waist. His fingers traced the silk rope that bound Rusty's hips and cock. He tugged at the knot to the rope. "I believe this has served its purpose." It loosened, and he gently pulled it from Rusty's cock.

Rusty groaned in relief, such as it was. The binding had done its job only too well. His dick was so hard it throbbed in time with his heartbeat.

Shiro's fingers delved under Rusty's robes, tracing the muscles along Rusty's sides, and then exploring Rusty's back. His breath caressed Rusty's ear. "I intend to do my best to bring you pleasure." His palms slid downward, following the line of red fur along his spine to the top of Rusty's tail.

Shiro's hands on his back felt so good. Rusty groaned and leaned forward against Shiro's powerful chest. He was so warm. He turned his nose into the frost silk of Shiro's hair. He smelled of sandalwood soap and masculine arousal. He smelled wonderful. He smelled like Shiro. He took another deep breath. "Can I have my hands back now?" His voice only sounded a touch desperate.

Shiro chuckled, a warm vibration against Rusty's heart. "Why?"

*Why?* Rusty pressed his lips to the side of Shiro's throat. "So, I can…touch you." On impulse, he stretched out his tongue to taste and explore the long muscle on the side of Shiro's throat from below his ear to his collarbone. He tasted slightly salty, and interesting.

Shiro trembled and groaned. "I think…not."

Rusty jerked his head back to stare into Shiro's hooded—and heated—gaze. "Why not?"

Shiro smiled and licked his lips. "Because…" He pressed his palm over Rusty's heart and pushed, firmly and steadily, forcing him to step backwards. "I am having a great deal of trouble controlling myself as it is."

Something came in contact with the back of Rusty's knees. Rusty turned to look, and felt a shove against his heart. Knocked off balance, he yelped and threw his arms up, but they were locked together at the thumbs.

Unable to stop himself, Rusty fell backwards, landing on his back with his hands over his head and his knees bent over the edge of the bed. Miraculously, his tail had curled to the side at the last second, so for once he didn't land on it. Sprawled across Shiro's bed with his hair tumbled about him and his robes spread open, Rusty gasped for breath.

Shiro licked his lips and smiled. "Oh, now that looks tempting." He set one knee on the edge of the bed, between Rusty's knees.

"Very funny!" Rusty tried to sit up, but it was awkward with his thumbs pinned together.

Shiro surged up on the bed between Rusty's knees, grabbing Rusty's wrist with one hand and pinning his arms up over his head. He smiled, his long silver mane spilling down, curtaining them both. "And where do you think you're going?"

Rusty stared up at Shiro, leaning over him, positioned between his knees. He licked his dry lips. "Uh…"

Shiro smiled, his hooded gaze burning. He leaned down and took Rusty's mouth in a devouring kiss.

Rusty groaned into Shiro's mouth, captured by the fierce and feral taste of Shiro burning on his tongue. *Good…* Anticipation sizzled through him, raising the small hairs all down his body. *Yes…* He shuddered and arched his back. *Yes…*

Shiro's tongue danced, his teeth nipped, and his lips caressed, but his body remained distant.

Rusty's hungry moans became whimpers of frustration. *More…* He dug his heels into the bed. *I need more…* He arched upward, striving to feel the sleek muscular body above him.

Abruptly, Shiro released Rusty's hands and sat back on his heels. He wiped his mouth with the back of his hand, his gaze narrowed and hot.

Shaking in a haze of aggravated lust, Rusty sat up, baring his teeth and growling, too furious to form a coherent thought.

Shiro smiled, showing all his long teeth. "That's what I've been waiting to see." He tugged at the knot to the decorative white cord binding his broad silver sash. The tasseled cord unknotted. He pulled it from his waist, and dropped it on the bed. "All that hidden passion finally unleashed."

# ~ *Twenty-Two* ~

SHIRO PLUCKED SOMETHING FROM WITHIN HIS BROAD SILVER SASH, THEN reached behind him to tug at the knot. "And so we begin." The silver silk parted and unraveled. He pulled it from his waist in a whispering rush and let it fall behind him to the floor. His blue and white robes parted, revealing his broad chest, muscular belly and the blushing curve of his cock. Moisture pearled and dripped from the tip. He tossed a small vial on the bed by Rusty's knee.

Rusty didn't even bother to look at the vial. The sight of Shiro proudly erect and only inches beyond his touch held his complete attention. He could smell Shiro's arousal, and all that delicious passion perfuming the air stirred a ravenous, instinctive need within Rusty; the need to grasp, and take.

He fisted his joined hands before him, and *wanted* them apart. Light flashed between his locked thumbs, and they parted.

Shiro gave a shout of laughter. "I see that someone has finally reached their limit." He eased backwards off the bed.

Shrugging out of his cumbersome robes, Rusty rolled forward onto his hands and knees. Digging his toes into the bed, his red tail straight out behind him, he stalked to the foot of the bed. He was not about to let his prey escape.

"That's it." Shiro dropped his robes to the floor, and backed away. "Come to me, my hungry one." He licked his lips and smiled with his ears forward, his thick white foxtail raised in a flag of challenge.

Rusty leaped, determined to take his prey to the floor.

Shiro lunged, meeting Rusty in mid-leap. Shiro's arms closed tight around Rusty's waist, his greater size and weight slamming Rusty backwards and onto the bed. Snarling, they grappled and rolled, legs entwined, each seeking to pin the other down to the bed.

Shiro proved difficult to hold. He slid through Rusty's hands like water. Somehow, Rusty ended up facedown on the bed with Shiro sitting on top of him, pinning his wrists to the small of his back.

Chuckling, Shiro reached over to collect the cord that had bound his sash from where it lay on edge of the bed, and then the vial he'd tossed earlier. "That comment you made earlier about bondage is proving accurate." He set the vial by his knee and then wound the cord around Rusty's wrists, binding them together. "I do indeed seem to be tying you up fairly often." He knotted the cords. "But then, you keep giving me such wonderful opportunities to do so."

Rusty bucked under him, snarling, his fury rendering him completely incapable of rational thought or speech.

"Yes, yes, I know you're hungry." Shiro nudged Rusty's anger-stiffened tail to one side and moved back off of Rusty's haunches to sit between his knees. "We'll get to that presently."

Rusty twisted sharply to the side.

"Oh, no, you don't." Shiro caught hold of Rusty's shoulders and pulled him between his splayed knees. He grabbed a fistful of the long red hair and closed his mouth on the wounds on the side of Rusty's throat.

Mind-searing pleasure arched Rusty's spine, and he gasped. His eyes closed and he moaned, his temper washed away under the drugging pleasure of Shiro's lips and hot velvety tongue.

His mouth locked to Rusty's throat, Shiro brought his hands together before Rusty's heart to remove the stopper to the vial. He tipped it, and a thick fluid spilled into Shiro's palm. He resealed the vial and tossed it aside, then pulled his hand back. Shiro delivered a final long lick to Rusty's wounds, then rose up on his knees and shoved Rusty forward.

With his hands tied behind him, Rusty barely turned his head in time to avoid being smothered by the blankets.

A hot palm pressed against Rusty's ass, right above the base of his tail, and rubbed in a slow circle.

Facedown on the mattress and ass in the air, Rusty gasped. The moving palm was somehow sending stimulation to his cock, his balls and his anus all at the same time. It wasn't exactly a feeling of friction, it was more like an outpouring of sensation, all from that one spot at the top of his ass.

Heat flushed his entire body and the line of fur on his spine rose. Sweat erupted all over his body. His back arched and tail lifted, then flopped over to the side. He couldn't stop his thighs from spreading wider. He groaned.

Shiro chuckled behind him. "Very sweet."

A slippery finger made contact with Rusty's anus and circled. He groaned and shivered. The finger on his anus didn't hurt, in fact the sensation was rather pleasurable, but it wasn't a pleasure he was used to feeling.

Pressure was applied to his anus, then increased. "Push out." Shiro's voice was husky and deep.

Confused by the sensations created by the hand moving on his ass above his tail and the pressure on his anus, Rusty pushed. A long, slick finger slid into his ass and circled within, inducing a vaguely pleasant tingling sensation.

The startling sensation mixed with the overwhelmingly sensual assault from the circling palm, and gasping moans burst from his throat. His body opened wider for the invading digit.

Shiro groaned. "You're so hot inside." A second finger entered and both slid deep to press against something within.

An excruciatingly exciting jolt clenched at the base of his balls, and then vibrated in his cock. Rusty released a startled gasp.

"Ah…" Shiro curled his fingers. "There it is." He rubbed back and forth slowly.

The fingers rubbing within him felt so good, Rusty moaned and his toes curled. It felt like he was going to cum, but it wasn't quite…hard enough. Unable to think past the need for more of that unbearably delicious sensation, he pushed back onto the fingers. Pleasure, yes, but still not quite enough. He surged forward and thrust back. He was rewarded with a bolt of pleasure that made him choke.

Shiro groaned and shifted. "Oh, you like that, do you?" He withdrew his fingers.

Rusty practically whimpered with the loss.

Shiro looped one arm around Rusty's hips and pulled Rusty back and up onto his knees against the broad wall of Shiro's chest. Suddenly the pressure on Rusty's anus was back, only harder, and hotter. Shiro groaned against the back of his neck. "Push out, hard."

Rusty pushed. Something violently hard, impossibly broad and incredibly hot spread his anus wide. The ache cleared his head fast. "Shit…" Shiro was trying to enter him. He groaned. "You're too big."

"No, I'm not." Shiro tightened his arm around Rusty's hips. "Push harder."

Rusty ground his teeth and pushed. Sweat dripped down his brow. His anus widened and Shiro's broad cock-head entered past the flared edge. It was almost a relief to feel himself close around the slightly narrower shaft. He released a long breath.

Shiro grunted and shoved. His cock slid deeper, and then deeper.

Rusty trembled. Shiro's cock was brutally hard. He arched back to relieve the ache, and suddenly felt pressure on that spot inside him. He gasped, and pushed against it.

Shiro gasped and surged all the way in. "Ah!"

Rusty shuddered and groaned. His butt felt so full, and yet there was that delicious pressure. At the same time, his tail and lower back were pressed against Shiro's belly in an oddly exciting manner. He trembled under a wash of confusing physical urges.

Shiro's fingers tugged at the rope around Rusty's wrists. "I need you to lean forward on your hands." He pulled the rope away, freeing Rusty's hands. "But don't touch yourself. I'll let you cum when I'm ready to let you cum."

*What?* Rusty trembled, caught between anger and need.

"Bastard…!"

"Yes, I know." Shiro rose under Rusty, pushing him forward. "Do it."

Rusty fell forward onto his hands.

Shiro rode him down, pressed against his back, his arm around Rusty's hips keeping them locked together.

The new position put greater pressure on that delicious spot within Rusty. He groaned and dropped to his elbows, shuddering, his fingers clenched in the sheets. His red hair spilled in a bright mass around him. He turned to look past his arm at Shiro.

Shiro pushed up on one hand. His mouth was tight, his bright copper gaze hooded, and his cheeks pink. "Remember, do not touch." He licked his lips, pulled back and thrust. Shiro's cock rammed right into that spot and surged beyond it, his hips slamming against Rusty's ass.

The vicious bolt of delight that burned through Rusty was very nearly more painful than the hard cock filling his ass, and just brutal enough to keep him from cumming right then. He released a choking cry.

Shiro froze over him. "Are you all right?"

Rusty groaned and shifted. "Fuck, I almost came."

"Ah…I thought you were that close." Shiro chuckled, and pressed a kiss to his shoulder. "That's why I told you not to touch." He withdrew, sliding lusciously past that spot only to thrust again, slamming back against it and surging past.

The exquisitely merciless jolt within forced another cry from Rusty's throat, and then another. That was what he wanted! He shoved back to meet the next thrust, and the next… The wickedly carnal pleasure increased in intensity, building to a boiling urgency.

Shiro's strokes came harder and faster, until his hips hammered against Rusty's ass with sharp damp smacks.

Mindless in his haze of excruciating ecstasy, Rusty gripped the sheets under him, slamming back into Shiro as hard as Shiro slammed into him, only dimly aware that he was ripping the fabric apart.

Shiro reached around Rusty's waist to close his hand around Rusty's cock. "Cum for me!" He pulled, stoking Rusty's cock with his thrusts.

Rusty shuddered. The breathtaking grip of Shiro's stroking hand combined with the savage delight stirred by the cock pumping in his ass. His choking cries became desperate shouts.

Overwhelmed, the hard, tight kick of orgasm ignited deep and low in his balls. Release erupted. He threw his head back and howled, taken by most severe climax he'd ever felt. The excruciatingly luscious sensation of liquid racing up his cock prolonged the cruel ecstasy, tearing more desperate sounds from his throat. His back arched and cum spattered the sheets.

Rusty collapsed on his side among the torn sheets, panting for breath and trembling from the force of his release. For several long seconds, the world went completely away.

Smiling, Shiro leaned over him. "Impressive. I almost came with you."

Rusty opened his eyes and groaned too tired to move. He looked blearily up at Shiro. "You didn't...?" He glanced down the length of his body. Shiro was still very hard, and seeping with his excitement.

Shiro brushed the damp hair from Rusty's brow. "You still have to feed." He sat back on his heels.

"Oh, jeez... Again?" Rusty groaned. "My ass...I don't think I can do it again."

"Oh, no?" Shiro smiled, reached down and grasped Rusty's cock. "You're still hard."

He *was* still hard, and the sensation of Shiro's hand on him was overpowering. Rusty's tail curled, and his knee came up in sheer reflex. He choked out a small cry before he could stop himself. "Don't...!"

Shiro caught him under the thigh and grabbed the very base of Rusty's tail. He lifted, turning Rusty onto his back.

Rusty yelped, and his tail curled up to cover his privates.

Shiro shoved Rusty's tail to one side and moved between Rusty's spread thighs. "I've kept you in a state of sexual excitement for several days." He leaned over him, his hands pressing into the mattress to either side. "Do you honestly think only one climax will release all of it?"

"And whose fault do you think that is?" Rusty curled his lip. "You sadist!"

"You know me so well!" Shiro smiled. "Actually, I wanted to exhaust some of that temper of yours before feeding you." His smile slid away. "You are dangerously close to true starvation." He cupped Rusty's face in his palms. "Feeding will not be pleasant for you."

Rusty flinched. His last feeding—that burning kiss—hadn't been pleasant at all.

Shiro leaned down and kissed his brow. "This time, you will have your fill."

Rusty looked up at him and glared. "Whether I want it or not?"

Shiro's gaze narrowed and his mouth tightened. "Correct."

# ~ Twenty-Three ~

GRASPING THE BACK OF RUSTY'S KNEES, SHIRO ROSE UP ON HIS KNEES, pushing Rusty's legs before him until Rusty rolled up onto his shoulders with his back completely off the bed, very nearly upside-down.

Startled, Rusty threw out his arms for balance and stared up at Shiro between his splayed knees. His ears folded down to the sides and his red, thick tail curled up against his side because it couldn't get between his legs. "Shiro? Ah, this is really, really…"

Shiro leaned over him between his spread thighs, clearly displaying that though Rusty was balanced practically on his head, he was in the perfect position to be fucked. "Are you in pain?"

Rusty's cheeks heated ferociously. "I'm embarrassed!" He groaned and tried to shift, but he couldn't move an inch.

"I need you to hold still so I can feed you." His gaze drifted toward the abandoned cord, still on the bed. His brows lifted. "I could bind you?"

"No!" He winced. He didn't want to sound desperate. "Uh, I'd rather…not be tied up." *Again.* He tried to shift his knees, but Shiro's grip on them was too tight.

Shiro shrugged slightly. "I don't know. I'd rather you didn't struggle, you could get hurt. Perhaps tying you might be best…?"

Rusty shivered and clutched at the sheets. "Please don't." Forget it, he *was* desperate.

Shiro smiled. "Are you going to be good?"

Rusty scowled. "What am I, a five-year old?"

"Some would say…" Shiro shrugged and glanced away. "There is a strong resemblance."

Rusty licked his lips. He really didn't want to fucked this way, and he really didn't want to be tied up either. "Shiro, please...? Can we do something else?"

"Can I trust you to submit?"

*Submit...* Rusty cringed. That sounded too much like *surrender.* But then, did he have a choice? He sighed. "You're absolutely, positive that we have to do this?"

Shiro's brows lowered and his mouth tightened. "You will die without feeding."

"Okay, but..." Rusty writhed, just a little. "Do I have to have all of it? Last time was a bit...much."

"You are the weakest among us. That makes you prey. Now, do you understand?"

Rusty stared up at Shiro. *Prey?* He decided that he really didn't want to know the full extent of what that could mean. "Oh."

Shiro's jaw tightened. "Then you'll accept your feeding without fighting me?"

Rusty's hands fisted in the torn sheets. He did not want to be anybody's *prey.* "Yes."

"Good." Shiro released Rusty's thighs, letting him flop sideways onto the bed. "That position would have grown tiring very quickly."

Rusty pushed up on his elbows, his mouth open in shock. "Then you never meant to...do it, that way?"

Shiro dropped down onto the tangled sheets, stretching out alongside Rusty, facing him. He smiled. "I assure you, I would have indeed fucked you exactly that way if you hadn't decided to cooperate."

"God!" Rusty turned his face into the sheets, then looked over at Shiro. "That was the most incredibly embarrassing position..."

Shiro delivered a breathtaking smile. "It's meant to be."

Rusty frowned at him. "You really *are* a sadist."

Shiro pressed a kiss to his brow. "But you love me anyway."

Rusty dropped his head on his arm and smiled. "Yeah, I noticed."

He rolled his eyes. "Somebody has to."

Shiro stilled utterly, and flames seemed to dance in the depths of his gaze. In a rush of hot flesh and white silky hair, Shiro grabbed the back of Rusty's head and took his mouth in a searing kiss that stole Rusty's breath.

Rusty moaned under the luscious torment of Shiro's tongue. He had no interest in resisting anymore. This was his future, as well as his past, all rolled into one incredible being of fire and frost and fur. And he loved him. Rusty closed his arms around Shiro's broad back and writhed against the hot steel of Shiro's muscular body, belly to belly and cock against cock.

Shiro broke the kiss and rose up on one elbow, licking his lips. "Now. I want you now."

Rusty dug his fingers into Shiro's hip. "Can we do it quick, before I panic?"

"We can." Shiro rose up on his knees, his cock a strong, arching column rising between his spread thighs, and his thick silver tail curled out to the side. He held out his hand. "Come."

Rusty knelt up to take Shiro's hand.

Shiro tugged Rusty close, then leaned back on one hand. "Mount."

Rusty blinked. "Huh?" He couldn't have heard that right.

Shiro smiled. "You wanted fast. Put me inside you and mount." He released Rusty's hand to lean back on his knees, resting on both palms.

Rusty swallowed. Gathering what shreds of courage he had left, Rusty leaned over Shiro and grasped his shoulder. The flesh was warm, hard and a little damp under his fingers. Rusty looked into Shiro's face and noticed that though Shiro's ears were up, his jaw was tight. Shiro was nervous, too. Somehow, that made it easier.

Rusty took a breath and lifted his leg over Shiro's lap to straddle him. He took a quick glance at Shiro's face.

The corner of Shiro's mouth had lifted in a slight smile.

*Okay...* Rusty released his breath. Keeping hold of Shiro's shoulder, he came down on his knees, practically sitting on Shiro's belly. He leaned back and had to release Shiro's shoulder. He set his palm over Shiro's heart and reached behind him to take hold of the strong smooth length of Shiro's cock. Thick moisture slicked his fingers from the seeping tip.

Shiro's entire body stiffened, his lips parted, and his eyes closed. He groaned. Beneath Rusty's palm, Shiro's heart pounded at a quickening pace.

Rusty stared and felt the hot curls of lust coil in his balls, stiffening his cock and making it weep. He licked his lips. This is what he wanted. He wanted to see Shiro just like this, desperate and coming apart.

Suddenly and violently, he wanted to see Shiro's face when he came, and he wanted him in his body when it happened. He rose up on his knees, and centered the hot and violently hard cock in his hand on his anus.

Before he could have second thoughts, he pressed down and pushed out. His body opened far more easily than it had the last time. He swallowed the broad head and almost half the length before he realized what happened.

Shiro gasped and released a deep, guttural moan.

A swift, hot bolt of triumph seared through Rusty. He threw back his head and pressed down, groaning, his body stretching to receive the heated length he'd shoved into it.

Shiro's arm came around Rusty's waist, his fingers digging into Rusty's ass, holding him steady.

Rusty grabbed hold of Shiro's strong, supporting arm and leaned back. He pressed down hard. Shiro's cock slid past that glory spot within him and he moaned. His ass settled on Shiro's thighs, fully impaled on his cock. He'd done it. He opened his eyes.

Shiro smiled, his gaze hooded and blazing with erotic fire. He leaned up and gripped the back of Rusty's neck, pulling him in for a breath-stealing kiss.

Rusty was forced to arch his back. It wasn't exactly comfortable, but damn it, he wanted to kiss Shiro. He wanted those silken lips moving against his. He wanted to feel the velvet rasp of his tongue, and taste his white-hot arousal.

Shiro's hand slid down to cup Rusty's ass. "Fuck me," he whispered against Rusty's lips. "Fuck me hard, and fast." His narrowed copper gaze shimmered like flames. He smiled. "Take me to heaven, love. Take us both."

Rusty licked his lips and delivered a shaky smile. "I'll do my best." He clutched Shiro's shoulders and rose up on his knees, repositioning his feet so he could dig his toes into the mattress. He took a deep breath and pushed, rising on the cock buried within him. The hot, smooth pleasure of withdrawal drew a sigh from his lips.

Shiro groaned, his lip curling and his body tensing under Rusty.

Rusty fell, and slammed down on his glory spot. The ferocious bolt of delight forced a small cry from his throat, searing him with the voracious need to feel it again. He dug his fingers into Shiro's shoulders and rose on the cock within him, then fell, taking it completely in one swift drop.

Beneath him, Shiro gasped and bucked, thrusting up to meet him.

Severe pleasure stabbed from behind his balls to the end of his dripping cock. Rusty shouted, "God, yes!" Enthralled by the vicious joy of a hard cock in his ass, Rusty rode, rising and falling, fucking himself mercilessly, his gasping shouts voicing his near-mindless delight.

Shiro rose and fell in swift hard counterthrusts, his fingers digging into Rusty's ass, his mouth open, his guttural shouts joining Rusty's.

The boiling surge of climax rose within Rusty, tightening into an unbearable knot almost frightening in its intensity. He froze for half a breath and gasped. "I'm...I'm going to cum."

Shiro shuddered under him, his jaw tensing and his eyes closing as though in pain. He leaned up on his knees, supporting Rusty by the ass with one hand, and grasped Rusty's cock with his other hand. "Cum, cum now!" He thrust, hard and fast, and pulled on Rusty's cock, stroking him in time with his thrusts.

Climax burst within, and agonizing rapture seared up Rusty's spine, forcing a howl from his throat. Cum surged into his cock in an exquisite rush and spilled, spattering musky cream across Shiro's belly.

Shiro knotted his finger in the hair at the base of Rusty's neck, and then he took Rusty's mouth in a ferocious kiss. Locking his arm around Rusty's hips, Shiro thrust violently, grinding up into Rusty's ass and then froze, buried to the hilt.

Locked to Shiro's mouth, and shuddering with tremors, Rusty felt Shiro's cock pulse within him, and then the thick, wet slide of Shiro's cum pumping into him. Fire exploded in his mouth and filled his ass, setting his spine and every nerve in his body alight with incandescence.

There wasn't time to scream.

Rusty awoke among a tangle of silk sheets with a hard, hot weight curled against his back, and a heavy arm around his waist. He opened bleary eyes. Gray light shimmered beyond gold and frost-white curtains.

He was in Shiro's bed. That was Shiro curled against his back. He'd done it. He'd finally delivered his body to Shiro. Not that Shiro had given him a whole lot of choice in the matter. *Sadistic bastard.*

It had been utterly terrifying, but incredible, too. A smile snuck onto his face, and he knew damned well that it was a stupid one. His butt was not particularly pleased, but the rest of him was. God, he hadn't thought it was even possible to cum like that.

Shiro loved him.

And he loved Shiro back. It was strange. It was wonderful. It was scary. He froze for two whole heartbeats. He was in love. Love with the big L. *Fuck!* He released his breath. He'd just have to learn to deal with it.

He glanced around the curtained bed. He was in a fairy-tale

palace, in the arms of a fairy-tale prince. A smile lifted the corner of his mouth. Okay, so a fairy-tale territorial governor.

His old life was well and truly over.

A strange pain surged in his heart. He had to close his eyes and hold his breath, just for a second or two.

The weight at his back shifted. Lips brushed against the back of Rusty's neck. "Good morning."

Rusty hastily wiped his cheeks and turned over. "Oh, hey."

"Hey." Shiro gave him a sleepy smile from under a tumble of silver hair, and it was breathtaking.

Rusty's heart caught on fire. He wanted to look away, but he just couldn't. Shiro was just too…beautiful.

Shiro's brows lifted and his smile disappeared. He lifted his hand and brushed a thumb across Rusty's damp cheek. "Are you all right?"

Rusty brushed his hand away. "I'm fine, it's…" *Nothing?* It wasn't 'nothing'. He took a sudden breath and decided to say what he felt. "You're just too cute to stand, you know that?"

"Cute?" Shiro blinked and then grinned. "Is that so?" He leaned up and dropped a swift kiss on Rusty's lips. "Personally, I think you're blindingly handsome."

Rusty smiled. "I think you're just plain blind, but who am I to complain?"

A loud rap sounded, and the chamber's door clicked open. "Your lordship?"

Shiro rolled his eyes and called out. "Yes, Chamberlain?"

The swift patter of slippers approached the bed.

Shiro sat up, and the sheets slithered away. "Never a day off, I swear…"

Rusty snatched for the sliding sheets, feeling incredibly self-conscious, though he wasn't quite sure why.

"Your lordship!" The curtains were pulled aside, revealing a smallish man, whose human-like head was nearly half the size of his body, in rather ornate robes. His eyes were huge and wide, as was his mouth. "Your lordship, have you looked outside?"

Shiro raised his knee and propped his arm up on it. "Chamberlain, in case you haven't noticed," he smiled, but his voice was very dry, "I haven't even gotten out of bed yet."

Chamberlain froze, blinked, then bobbed a swift bow toward Shiro. "Oh, of course, excuse me." He nodded toward Rusty. "Good morning."

His cheeks burning, Rusty nodded back. "Good morning."

Chamberlain stepped back from the bed. "If you would just come to the balcony, your lordship?"

Shiro waved his hand. "Fine, bring me a robe."

Chamberlain pattered off.

Shiro turned to Rusty. "You'll be seeing a lot of him." He leaned close and whispered. "Palace tattle-tale."

Rusty smiled in spite of himself. "Oh, is that how it is?"

Shiro shrugged. "Well, technically, that's his job."

The patter of slippers returned. Draped across his arms, Chamberlain held out a velvet robe of midnight blue. "Your lordship."

Shiro frowned at the robe, then stood up, completely at ease with his nudity, and shrugged into it. He knotted the tie. "So what exactly, is the problem?"

"This way, your lordship..." Chamberlain trotted off past the bed, obviously to the balcony doors.

Shiro followed.

There was a click, then a creak. An icy breeze washed into the room.

"Fuck!" The shout came from Shiro.

Rusty froze.

"Rusty! Get your ass over here!"

There wasn't a robe in sight, so Rusty gathered up the sheet and wound it around his waist.

"Rusty!"

"Give me a sec, I'm naked here!" He knotted the sheet and headed around the bed to the glass doors behind it. Unlike last night, they were all closed but one. He strode for the open door.

Outside on the balcony, Shiro stood in his midnight blue velvet, his arms folded across his chest and his long white mane blowing in the freezing wind, blending perfectly with the snow swirling from the softly glowing sky.

*Snow?* Rusty crossed his arms over his bare chest, and stepped barefoot into a good four fingers worth of snow. He leaned over the balcony railing and watched the snow fall into the mist below. "Holy shit!" Last night it had been warm enough to be outside, this morning it was snowing? The weather sure did change fast around here.

The chamberlain danced from foot to foot. "We don't know how this happened your lordship, but it's all over the mountain and edging into the next district!"

"Oh, I know exactly what happened." Shiro narrowed his eyes at Rusty.

The chamberlain bobbed. "Oh, you do? Oh, that's excellent!"

*Me?* Rusty pointed at his own chest. *I did this?*

Shiro's brow lifted and his smile tightened.

*Shit...* Rusty groaned and looked back over the balcony at the snow. He hadn't done it on purpose! He smiled just a little. But it was rather pretty.

Shiro nodded at the chamberlain. "Please tell the staff that I'll take care of this at once."

"Of course, your lordship." The chamberlain bowed and stepped back into the bedroom.

Shiro reached out and grabbed Rusty by the arm. "You." He shoved Rusty backwards toward the door. "Get your ass inside, now."

"Hey!" Rusty backpedaled, tripping over his trailing sheet.

Shiro followed Rusty inside, closed the glass door and faced the chamberlain. "Would you be so kind as to send a message to Master Cloud at the School of the Elements and tell him we have someone in dire need of an education?" He brushed the snow off his sleeves and shot a narrowed glare at Rusty. "Mark it urgent."

The chamberlain bowed. "Yes, your lordship, at once, your

lordship." He turned on his heel and pattered for the chamber door.

Shiro pointed a long finger at Rusty. "You need to learn how to control your passions!" He set his hands on his hips, and scowled at Rusty. "This is the second time you made a snowstorm, and this time you did it in *my* district."

"What?" Rusty backed away from him. "It's not like I did it on purpose!"

"No shit." Shiro shrugged out of his blue robe and tossed it on the end of the bed. "Get back on the bed."

Rusty clutched at the sheet around him. "Are you going to tie me up again?"

Shiro grinned, showing all his long teeth. "I'm going to spellbind your weather-working ass, so yes, in a manner of speaking."

*Shit...* Rusty backed away, but his cock was already getting hard. "In bed?"

"Yes." Tall, gorgeous, and utterly naked, Shiro stalked after Rusty. "If I have to chase you, I'm going to do a lot more than just bind you with spellwork."

Rusty grinned. "God, I hope so!"

Shiro froze, then barked out a laugh. He scraped a hand through his long hair and smiled. "This is certainly going to be an interesting relationship."

Rusty snorted. "I wouldn't want you to have a dull moment."

Shiro rolled his eyes. "I honestly don't think it's possible."

Rusty nodded. "Good." He dropped his sheet and bolted.

Shiro lunged after him.

Laughter and yelps filled the chamber for quite some time after that.

~ * ~

# Also by Morgan Hawke

## Excerpt from TORRID - A Shounen-Ai/Yaoi Romance

*P*anting and sweating, Trey leaned against the metal wall of the huge stall and peeled his boots off, scattering crushed and wadded bills everywhere. He smiled. Apparently he was a hit. He didn't bother to count it, just pulled his folded clothes out of his bag and stuffed all the money in as-is. He'd un-wad all of it and count it once he got home.

Barefoot and wearing only his g-string, he padded over to the sinks to try and get some of the sweat and goop off before he climbed back into his clothes.

Unfortunately, the lube proved difficult to get off. A lot of wet paper towels and handfuls of the bathroom's poor excuse for soap later, he finally realized that it was going to take a shower to get the vanilla scent off his skin.

He groaned. He was going to smell like a freaking pudding cake all the way home. He scowled at the wasted paper towels. "Shit."

"Damn, something smells good enough to eat in here." The voice was masculine and very familiar.

At the sink, soapy paper towels in hand, Trey froze. He closed his eyes. *No way... He did not follow me in here.* He opened his eyes and turned.

The guy smiled from the doorway. "You were right; you *are* a damned good dancer."

*Oh, shit...* Trey smiled weakly. "Um, thanks."

The guy sniffed and frowned. "What in God's name...? Is that vanilla smell, you?"

Trey felt his cheeks heat and looked down at the sink. "I'm sensitive to oils, so I used..." No way, he was going to say lube. "I used something else, and it's vanilla flavored." *What am I saying?* He looked up at the guy in shock. "Scented! Vanilla scented!"

"Is that so?" The guy grinned and approached, his gait slow and easy, a stalking predator. "I don't know. You smell pretty tasty to me."

Watching him closing in, Trey's heart thumped in his mouth. *I think I am in serious trouble here.* He swallowed.

"I think I should check and see." The guy's brows lifted. "Take a taste-test."

*A taste test...?* Trey sucked in a breath, dropped the paper towels in his hand and backed away. "Uh, let's not, okay?"

The guy's smile sharpened, showing very white and very even teeth. "After that display up on the stage, right in front of God and everybody, now you're shy?"

Trey backed into the wall. "How about—not gay?"

The guy snorted. "Good, me neither." He lunged.

# ~ One ~

"This historical mansion is supposed to be haunted. Isn't that cool?"

Thunder boomed, rattling the rattan frames of the long, rice paper sliding walls on the left.

"What?" The rubber soles of Keiko's pink house slippers caught on the antique red and gold carpet, making her trip. She barely kept from pitching into the student directly in front of her. With the entire class crammed in the narrow hallway, there was barely enough walking room, never mind room to fall. She turned to her left, and frowned at her classmate. "Tika, did you say the house is *haunted*?"

"Yep." Tika smiled, showing the boy-grabbing dimple in the heart of her cheek. The light shining through the warm cream of the rice paper wall on their left gave her oval face a warm glow. "The ghost of an old samurai is supposed to be watching over the family."

Keiko winced. "Great." Her class *would* arrange a *haunted* house tour during an autumn storm. She wiped her damp palms down the black jacket emblazoned with the university's logo over her left pocket. Her hooded slicker had saved her hair and blazer from getting soaked, but the hem of her plain black skirt and her stockings were still damp.

Suddenly, the rest of Tika's comment sank in. Keiko turned to frown at her. "The ghost is watching over the family? Are you saying they're in residence? They still live here?"

"Yep." Tika put on a grim expression, and lifted her finger in imitation of their instructor. "This is a private tour granted to the university by the highly esteemed house owner; a very respectable alumni." She leaned close to Keiko's ear. "And I hear that the son, and heir to the family company, is currently attending, and…" She winked. "He's supposed to be really cute, too!"

Keiko frowned in confusion. "Where'd you hear all this?"

Tika rolled her eyes and shook her head, her sleek black hair falling into a perfectly trimmed wedge at her chin. "It was in the documentation passed out in class. Didn't you read it?"

"Yes, I read…some." Keiko's cheeks heated. Actually, she hadn't read any. "I was working on my essay." She fiddled with the plain black ribbon tie around the collar of her white blouse. "I missed the bit about the ghost." She glanced around, but saw nothing unusual about the rattan-framed sliding walls on her left, or in the paintings hanging on the polished cedar wall on her right. "How big is this house?" *How long is this tour?*

"Really freaking huge; I bet we'll be walking all day." Tika sighed and reached out to stroke the rice-paper wall they were passing with her fingertips. "On top of that, with all the sliding walls in this place, it's more of a maze than a mansion. Someone is bound to get lost."

"Not me." Keiko had absolutely no desire to wander away from her fellow students; not in a haunted house. She peered over the shoulders of the students ahead of her.

A tall man in a gray, military-style uniform leaned casually against the polished cedar wall on the right, as though he was some kind of guard. His arms were folded, defining muscle normally hidden under long sleeves. His sleek black hair was tucked behind his ears and a little overlong, falling just past his nicely broad shoulders. The tailored cut of his gray coat showed a flat stomach and narrow hips.

Keiko sucked in a breath. *Damn…* Whoever he was, he was seriously fine.

He lifted his chin and scanned up the line of students.

Keiko turned her head so he wouldn't notice her impolite staring, and peeked from the corner of her eye. His uniform looked familiar, but she couldn't quite place where she'd seen it before.

The line stopped, only two students away from the man against the wall. No one looked at him; not even a glance.

Keiko frowned.

Tika sighed and started cataloguing just how handsome her latest boyfriend was. Her favorite subject.

Keiko smiled, then turned slightly away, rolling her eyes. Tika would probably be chatting non-stop for the next hour. Her gaze drifted to the man in gray against the wall. Not one student looked his way, as though they just didn't notice him standing there.

*Weird.* Curling a finger around the end of her long black ponytail, Keiko looked over at her schoolmate.

Tika was deep into describing the perfection of her boyfriend's butt, grinning and gesturing enthusiastically with her hands.

Keiko's brows lifted. Tika wasn't noticing the guy against the wall either, and that was really strange. He was blindingly handsome. There was no way she would have been able to resist flirting with him. What was going on? She turned back to look at him.

His face was...perfect, not too angular, not too oval, and he had a mouth to die for--but there was not one drop of color in his face, or in anything he wore. He looked as though he had stepped from an old black and white film.

Keiko suddenly realized where she'd seen that uniform. Although it was gray, rather than black, she was clearly looking at a military uniform from over a hundred years ago. She felt a far too familiar humming inside the back of her head, and the hairs at the back of her neck lifted.

She was staring at a ghost.

He turned and looked straight at her. His midnight eyes under straight black brows danced with flickers of unearthly blue fox-fire. He unfolded his arms and straightened, his eyes narrowing. "You see me." His voice caressed the inside of her head with the warmth of late summer, and the perfume of faded chrysanthemums.

Keiko jerked her gaze away and grabbed onto Tika's arm.

Tika yipped, then grinned. "What? Did you see the ghost?"

Keiko dug her fingers into Tika's arm. "No."

A summery chuckle echoed across her thoughts. "Yes…"

Keiko cringed, and peeked from the corner of her eye.

He was gone.

"Take it easy with the death-grip, will you?" Tika shrugged out of Keiko's hold, then smiled. "If you're that scared, I'm sure I can find a guy to hold your hand?"

Keiko clasped her hands behind her. "No, thanks, I was just startled." Guys were even more trouble than ghosts.

Tika raised a perfectly manicured brow. "If you're sure…?"

"I'm fine, really." Keiko gave her a big fake smile and jaunty wave.

The professor, at the very head of the double line of students, lifted his arms to signal that the tour was turning down a hallway on the right. He began droning on about the esteemed house's artworks. The students directly ahead moved forward.

Tika tugged on Keiko's sleeve. "Go, go, go!"

Keiko rolled her eyes. "I'm going! I'm going!" Her slippers slapping on the carpet and her long black ponytail swinging against her back, she trudged after the student before her. She was very careful to look away from where the ghost had been standing.

Thunder crashed overhead, rattling the paper walls.

Keiko looked up toward the ceiling. The dangling Victorian era light fixture swayed slightly overhead.

Tika gasped, tripped and fell hard against Keiko's left side.

Keiko toppled over toward the cedar wall on her right, and threw out her hands, falling… She landed on her shoulder and sprawled on the floor. Groaning, she sat up, rubbing her aching shoulder. "Thanks a lot, Tika." She froze. Right in front of her, where Tika and the rest of her class should have been, was a cedar wall--and no door.

She gasped, and looked up. The shadowed ceiling was very far away and artfully draped in magnificent sheets of scarlet and gold silk. She twisted around on her butt and discovered that she was sitting on the floor at the far end of a long and deeply shadowed audience chamber. The walls were lined with gigantic wall screens embroidered in brilliant rainbow hues and illuminated from behind.

"What…?" She scrambled to her feet. "How did I get here?" The hair on her neck lifted and the back of her head shimmered with awareness.

"You fell through the door." The voice came from right behind her.

Her breath caught and her hands turned to ice. She whirled.

The gray man, the ghost, was directly behind her less than a foot away, leaning against the cedar wall with his arms crossed. He smiled, and blue flames blazed in the midnight depths of his eyes. "I am Ryudo. Welcome to my home."

Keiko sucked in a deep breath, turned on her heel and bolted. Her slippers slapped loudly on the woven *tatami* mats fitted across the floor. She skidded to a stop near the wall screen at the opposite end of the huge empty room. There had to be a door somewhere.

Near the left wall a seam of light spilled across the shadowed floor from between two screens. A sliding door.

She lunged for it.

The screens slammed together.

Keiko jerked to a halt, her heart slamming in her chest. A shimmer of awareness tingled at the back of her skull. *Ghost...* She backed away from the door. Her back came in contact with the opposite screen. It slid under her hands. She turned and pulled on the bamboo frame. The wall parted, revealing a window.

She stuck her head out onto a dark cross-hallway. No lights were lit and no one was in sight. Windows lined the entire opposite wall. Beyond the glass, rain fell on a magnificent walled-in, outdoor garden, complete with shrines and fountains. The storm's wind tossed the branches of the carefully pruned trees, and blown leaves stuck to the wet glass. Thunder rumbled.

A sigh came from behind her, and the scent of faded flowers.

Keiko charged into the hallway. Something caught the collar of her coat, trapping her in the doorway.

"Going somewhere?"

Keiko gasped, barely stopping her scream. She tugged, but her coat was caught fast. She wriggled out of it, and plunged into the hallway. Her slippers skidded on the slippery, waxed wood floor, and she nearly crashed into the window across the hall. She turned around. The door she had just emerged from was gone, and her coat with it. She faced one long wall of identical bamboo-framed panels.

She stepped out into the middle of the hall with no clue which way she should go, left or right. Both ways led to a blind corner. There was not a sound but wind and rain. She was lost--in a haunted house.

She turned to her right and took a hesitant step.

Thunder rumbled, then lightning flashed beyond the windows. Shadows from the tossing branches moved in the hallway around her. Six long paces ahead of her, in the center of the hallway, something shimmered in the air. The shimmer coalesced into Ryudo.

Keiko's breath stopped. She backed away. "Why are you chasing me?" Stupid question, she knew good and well why ghosts chased her.

Ryudo's black brows lifted. "Why are you running away?"

Keiko kept backing up. "You're a ghost."

Ryudo scowled. "I assure you, my...status of being was not my choice." He stepped toward her.

Keiko whirled and bolted. Her slippers flew off her feet. She let them go and kept running in her stocking feet. Sliding across the waxed floor, she grabbed the corner and hurled herself around the right-hand turn. She skidded into a long gallery filled with standing glass cases crammed with vases, brass statuary and funeral urns. The hall was dark but for the lights within the cases.

Keiko hurried along the slippery floor past the displays, trying not to slide into any of the cases while searching for a door. There had to be a door. The end of the hall was a left hand turn, and then another long gallery of cedar walls lined with silk paintings. This hall was even darker than the last, but light shown at the left turn at far end. She scooted into the hall.

Thunder rumbled, and the scent of chrysanthemums whispered in the air.

"Don't go. Stay."

Something pulled at the tie in her hair. She didn't think, she shook her head and lunged into the dark hallway. Her long black hair loosened from the tie, tumbling free down her back to her waist.

"Ah... Very nice."

Keiko turned the corner, gasping for breath, and found another cedar-walled hallway. This one was very narrow, and lined with antique silk robes under glass. The light came from the cases. Her legs shaking, she walked as fast as she could. All this running was seriously beginning to tire her out.

A shimmer appeared at the end of the hall.

Keiko stopped dead, then backed away.

Ryudo coalesced with his hands behind his back. His booted feet were clearly not touching the floor. "Are you ready to stop running?"

Keiko scowled, and kept backing away. This game of his was getting on her nerves. "Are you ready to stop chasing me?"

"My pursuit will end when you stop running." He tilted his head, and pursed his full, colorless lips. "Though I will admit, I haven't been this entertained in quite a while."

Keiko stopped, her hands fisting at her sides. "You think this is *fun*?"

Ryudo's brows lifted. "Pursuing the attentions of a pretty girl?" He gave her a breathtaking smile. "Absolutely." He raised his hand, and gestured.

The black ribbon tie around Keiko's collar fell out of its snug bow. She stared down at her loosened tie. "What...?"

"The only thing I find more entertaining ..." Ryudo made a snatching motion with his hand. "Is undressing one."

The ribbon slithered off her neck in a whisper of silk and sailed across the room to his hand. Keiko gasped in shock. "My tie!"

Ryudo tilted his head. "Aren't you a little warm, all buttoned up like that?" He gestured again.

The top button at the throat of Keiko's white blouse popped open. "Hey!" Keiko grabbed for her shirt. "Stop that! You...pervert!"

He blinked. "Pervert?" A completely masculine smile lifted his lips, and pale blue fox-fire gleamed in the heart of his black eyes. "I can show you perversion, if you like." He lifted both of his hands.

*Oh, shit!* Keiko turned and bolted back down the hall. She spotted an inch-wide crack in a seam in the left wall, between two *kimono* displays, and grabbed for it. The wall slid open to the left. She didn't look, she just squeezed through.

Keiko found herself in another dark gallery, this one with murals embroidered in silk hanging along the right wall, with rice-paper walls lining the left. She groaned. Tika had been right. The house was a freaking maze.

Rain could be heard pattering against the roof tiles.

Keiko looked up. She had to be close to the outside.

The hint of summer heat and flowers washed across her thoughts. "Wait, I was just starting to get to know you."

"Yeah, right." Keiko glared at the ceiling, and marched up the hall with determination. "By taking off my clothes?"

"I was merely curious." Soft laughter echoed. "Would you like to know what's under mine?"

Keiko's imagination suddenly filled with an image of a strong masculine chest, silky black hair falling across broad shoulders, and a stomach defined by sleek muscle. She shook her head. *What am I thinking? He's a ghost!* But he did have nice-looking hands, and a mouth to die for… *No.* She would not even consider…what his butt really looked like. She ground her teeth, and forcibly slammed a lid on her wayward imagination. "No, thank you!"

Warm, summery chuckles followed her down the hallway.

# About the Author

" *For* me, writing is more than a passion, it's an *obsession*."

Morgan Hawke has been writing erotic fiction since 1998. She has lived in seven states of the US and spent two years in England. She has been an auto mechanic, a security guard, a waitress, a groom in a horse-stable, in the military, a copywriter, a magazine editor, a professional tarot reader, a belly-dancer and a stripper. Her personal area of expertise is the strange and unusual.

Ms. Hawke maintains a close and personal relationship with her computer and her cat.